Marrying
Off MOM

Marrying Off MOM

Martha Tolles

AN
APPLE
PAPERBACK

SCHOLASTIC INC.
New York Toronto London Auckland Sydney

To Favorite Fathers
Roy, Steve, and Alex

ISBN 0-590-42843-8

12 11 10 9 8 7 6 5 4 3 2 1   0 1 2 3 4 5/9

Printed in the U.S.A.

First Scholastic printing, February 1990

Contents

1.
Good News and Bad

Kim Conway followed her mother through the back-to-school-night crowds and looked around eagerly for her friends. She was dying to talk to them because tonight was the night. She'd been waiting for it ever since school started.

But as she hurried through the crowds of mothers and fathers and boys and girls, a wave of sadness swept over her. For a moment it seemed as if her dad were there again. She could almost imagine that he was walking beside her and talking to her in that deep voice of his.

Instead, she heard a voice calling, "Kim, Kim!" She whirled around and saw Angie, with her frizzy dark hair and her smiling brown eyes, coming toward her.

Kim rushed to meet her friend. "Angie, hi! I've been looking for you. Do you think my plan is going to work out for tonight?"

"Sure, of course." Angie grinned. "Does your mom know about it yet?"

"Well, not exactly. I have to be careful what I tell her about things like this." Kim shook her head despairingly. "I couldn't get her to wear her plum-colored dress, either. She *insisted* on staying in the beige suit that she wore to the office." Kim had tried for weeks to get her mom to grow her hair longer, too, or at least her fingernails, and to paint them a bright color, but no luck.

"Well, don't worry, Kim." Angie was comforting. "Looks aren't everything."

Just then, there came a shriek of laughter from behind them. They turned to see a bunch of girls clustered around the dark-haired new boy, Mike Martines. One of the girls, tall and blonde, was saying loudly, "You should see my bike. It's the absolute best. My dad and I built it."

"Listen to that Lorraine," Angie said disgustedly. "She's always boasting about something."

"I know." Kim frowned. "And handing out advice, too. Can you believe it, that she's moved in next door to me?" Lorraine was someone they'd both known at school for a long time but never really liked. "Anyway, at least Mike Martines moved onto my street, so that almost makes up for it."

"He couldn't be that great," Angie scoffed. "Lorraine's a lot to make up for. Just look at her!"

But Kim was peering up the hall, looking for her mother. She saw her slight figure up ahead.

"I better go, Angie. You do think my idea for my mom is good, don't you?"

"Of course," Angie agreed. "Besides, everybody likes Mr. Chang."

Kim felt hopeful as she started off up the hall. But even from here she could see such a difference between her mom and the other parents, who were all talking and laughing and calling out to one another. Her mom's face looked sad as she stood, waiting in that quiet way of hers, and the same old worry darted through Kim's mind — was her mom ever going to be happy again?

"Sorry, Mom." Kim hurried up to her mother. "I just had to talk to Angie for a minute. Come on, let's go this way." She tucked her hand under her mom's elbow and steered her in the direction of her sixth-grade classroom. Of course, Kim was eager to show her mom her schoolwork, her book report with the A on it, for instance, but most of all she was excited about this big chance at last for her mom to meet Mr. Chang.

"I think you'll really like my teacher, Mom," she said earnestly. "He's nice, and smart, too." For weeks Kim had been telling her mom all these good things about him.

"I'm so glad you're happy with him, Kim, dear. Dad would've been so proud of you." Mrs. Conway's face began to look sad again.

"I know, Mom, I know." Kim wished her mom

wouldn't talk about her dad. She didn't want them to start thinking about him right now. They'd both just get sad and remember other back-to-school nights when he was here with them. "Come on, Mom," she said as they turned into the classroom. "I'll introduce you to Mr. Chang."

But lots of mothers and fathers and kids were already squeezed around Mr. Chang, and others were standing in line, waiting their turn.

"Let's get in line, too," Kim said. She didn't dare say how much she hoped her mom and Mr. Chang would like each other. But it could happen, couldn't it? They might get to talking, then her mom would invite him over for dinner. If not, maybe Kim would suggest something like Mr. Chang coming over for a barbecue for instance. Her mom would say, "Yes, yes, what a good idea." Or they could even have take-out Chinese food, which was one of her mom's favorites. Would Mr. Chang like that, too?

But Kim didn't think she should mention any of this now. "I'll go get my books and my book report to show you," she said, and she went over to her desk and got out her schoolwork.

Her mother was pleased with the book report and looked at all of Kim's papers and books while they waited in line. Kim kept glancing around the room, hoping to see Mike Martines, hoping that

4

he wasn't still out in the hall with Lorraine. It was such good luck that he was in her class, too.

Just then, Kim saw her friend Sara come into the classroom with her mother. Kim and Sara waved to each other. Sara's mom was wearing enormous hoop earrings and a bright red jacket, and her face had a kind of lighted up, happy look to it. Kim thought she looked terrific, and she couldn't help a quick glance at her own mother, who had brown hair and quiet blue eyes and tiny silver earrings that hardly showed at all. If only her mom could wear clothes that were a little more stylish!

But now the line was moving, and they were reaching the head of it. Somehow, Lorraine and her parents had come into the room and were suddenly standing right behind them. Kim ignored them.

"Hi, Mr. Chang." Kim smiled happily at her teacher and took in a deep breath. The big moment had finally arrived. "Mom, this is Mr. Chang. This is my mom," she added.

"Hello, Kim. How's everything? Glad to meet you, Mrs. Conway." He smiled at Kim's mom, who smiled back. But then, for some strange reason, he peered through his glasses at Lorraine's dad. "Is this your dad?"

"Oh, no!" Kim exclaimed, horrified. "Uh . . ."

Then she thought, Why not let Mr. Chang know that her mom is a widow and available. "I don't have a father."

"That's right," Mrs. Conway added in a low voice. "Kim's father died nearly three years ago in a car accident. There're just the three of us now, counting Kim's younger brother."

Kim was sorry her mom had mentioned her brother. Two children might be just a little much, might scare Mr. Chang off.

"I'm sorry." Mr. Chang looked slightly flustered, but so kind and sympathetic, Kim thought her mom was sure to like him. Then he added, "These automobile accidents are really terrible, aren't they? My wife and I've had several friends involved in them lately."

Kim felt a wave of disappointment sweep over her. His wife? He had a wife. Somehow she'd thought he didn't, maybe because he never mentioned his family in class. So all these weeks of hoping and planning were just a waste. Kim was so disappointed that she stopped listening and let the words flow past her.

Suddenly, she realized Mr. Chang was looking at her and saying, "I have a lot of good things to say about Kim. She's doing very good work."

"Thanks, Mr. Chang." Kim managed to feel a small glow of pleasure.

"Yes, and we're going to do an interesting research project this year. We'll be having a career contest, and the students will write reports about different kinds of jobs. The winners will be photographed and written up in the local paper."

Kim felt a burst of excitement in spite of her recent disappointment. "How terrific!" she exclaimed. "What — "

A loud voice interrupted from behind her. "A career contest? Oh, Mr. Chang, how great. I have the best idea for one." Lorraine pushed forward and planted herself right in front of Kim. "Here are my parents, right back here, my dad and . . ."

So that was the end of their talk with Mr. Chang. But in a way, it didn't matter, Kim consoled herself later as she and her mom made their way down the hall through the crowds. The meeting with Mr. Chang hadn't worked out the way she'd hoped. There wouldn't be any barbecue in their backyard with him after all. But at least Kim knew she was really going to like being in Mr. Chang's class. As for her mom, well there must be other men somewhere in the world for her to meet.

2.
Dwayne From the Office

Something happened sooner than Kim had expected. Just as she and her mother were driving home from back-to-school night that evening, her mother said, "Kim, I have a very busy day tomorrow. Late in the afternoon a man named Dwayne Higby is coming by the house to see me."

Kim stopped looking out the window and thinking about Lorraine Ridley. She'd been wondering what great idea Lorraine had for her career report. She turned to stare at her mom's profile in the darkness as Mrs. Conway turned their car onto Palm Street.

"Really, Mom? Is he coming for a special reason?" Right away Kim began to feel excited. Did it have anything to do with the real estate office where her mother worked as a secretary? Or was it better than that?

But her mom said, "It's nothing much. He may arrive before I get home from work. Would you be sure to straighten up the living room right after school?" Her mother's tone of voice shut out more questions.

With a twist of the steering wheel, she steered their car up the driveway and into the garage, and snapped off the lights. Kim wanted to ask more, but she knew her mom didn't like to be bothered with questions like, Why didn't she have dates the way Sara's mom did, or, Why didn't she go out more to singles parties, and so on. Still, Kim couldn't help blurting out, "Sara's mom has a new boyfriend." She felt a pang of envy just thinking about it. Sara had told her all about the new boyfriend, how her mother had met him while she was at work as a hostess in a restaurant. "Sara says he's really fun."

"Kim," Mom said warningly as she stepped out of the car. "You aren't going to start badgering me again, are you?"

"But Sara's mom — "

"Please, dear, not tonight. It's been hard enough remembering how Dad used to be here with us at other back-to-school nights. It's been a difficult evening."

Kim fell silent then because she knew what her mother meant. It had brought back the memories and the sad feelings. She followed her mother through the darkness to the lighted kitchen door. From inside drifted the murmur of TV voices from the living room, where Mrs. Greenberg, who lived next door to them, would be waiting on the couch. Mrs. Greenberg used to sit for them a lot, but that was back in the old days when they still had a dad.

But now she hardly ever came, and things were pretty quiet around their house, especially if Randy was asleep. It wasn't like Angie's home, where her father and mother joked and watched football on TV or cooked large meals together for Angie and her brothers. It wasn't like Sara's, either, where her mother and her mother's boyfriend ate dinner by candlelight. And it wasn't the way Kim's used to be. Kim could still remember her dad's and mom's friends coming for barbecues in the backyard. She knew she would never forget those happy times.

"How's the job going, Mrs. Conway?" Mrs. Greenberg stood up and began pulling on her jacket over her purple jogging suit. She often went walking and always wore bright-colored jogging suits.

Kim's mom sighed. "Pretty well, thank you, Mrs. Greenberg."

The white-haired woman shook her head. "I know you've got lots on your shoulders these days, what with these two kids to raise and all, and prices are real high, aren't they? Even the price of cat food for my Peter has gone sky-high."

Kim went on down the hall to her bedroom, not wanting to hear more about how things were so tough for her mom and all of them now. She knew that already, how things had changed after that night of her dad's accident. That was back three years ago, when she was only eight years old. She'd never forget that night when the telephone rang, the way her mom clutched the phone, her face turning pale. A drunk driver had swerved across the road and smashed into Mr. Conway's car.

For months afterwards, Kim would think she'd hear her dad moving around the house at night, his heavy footsteps, his deep voice. Or she'd almost believe she'd find him sitting in the big chair in the living room, reading his newspaper. Sometimes, even after she was in bed, she'd get up and go peek down the hall. He had to be in the living room. He was just being extra quiet, that's all. But he was never there, of course. Oh, it wasn't fair what had happened. Kim began to undress and blinked her eyes hard, thinking of that bad time. She'd hated the other driver for such a long time for crashing into her dad like that. But he'd been killed, too.

Kim went to her closet to get her pajamas. She remembered how she and her mom used to talk and talk on the phone with Uncle Rick and Aunt

Ruth back in Boston. They'd say, "Let go of the bitterness and the memories. Try to move on. Think about the living." Kim thought they had tried to do that, too. And her mom had joined an organization to fight drunk driving, and every month sent a small contribution. "At least that might help prevent someone else from having an accident," Mrs. Conway had said.

Now Kim pulled on her pajamas and wished she hadn't started remembering all this again. She'd think about now, today instead, like Mike Martines moving onto her street.

She paused in front of the mirror to stare into her blue eyes, blue like her mom's eyes. Mike's moving here was the good part, she told herself, and being in Mr. Chang's class, and so was the career contest, if only she could write a top report. But having that Lorraine Ridley next door was not so great.

Kim climbed into bed, snapped off her bedside lamp, and stared at the darkness. Now her mind went back to her mother again. Kim thought about Dwayne Higby coming tomorrow and slipped into her favorite fantasy. Maybe he'd make her mom smile and laugh, and she would start to date, like Sara's mom. One day they'd get married and he'd even look like their old dad, the way her dad was in that photograph on her mother's bureau. Of course, they'd never find a dad as good as their real one. Second best would have to do. But her mom would start acting happy again, and things would be the way they used to be, with a mother and a father. They'd be a real family again.

3.
Spring Passion Perfume

Kim uncapped the Spring Passion perfume she had given her mom for Christmas and held it beneath her nose. She breathed deeply. But the perfume tickled her nose, so she put it down quickly.

Then she moved the perfume right next to her mother's hairbrush, so her mother would have to see it. Then she paused by her dad's framed picture. "You'd think it was all right, wouldn't you, Dad? Mom's so sad, you see." She stared into the still eyes in the photograph, trying to imagine what he'd say about all this. He'd want her mother and all of them to be happy, wouldn't he? She leaned toward her reflection in the mirror to ask herself the same question. But could this girl with curly brown hair and blue eyes give her the answer?

She heard the front door bang, and she hurried out of the room and down the hall. "Hi, Mom." Mrs. Conway was crossing the living room, unbuttoning her jacket and looking around. "I've already dusted." Kim had picked up Randy's toys, vacuumed the green rug, and watered the fern in the window.

Her mother nodded. "Looks good, Kim, dear. Thanks."

"How soon is he coming?" Kim asked.

"Right away." Mrs. Conway started down the hall. "I'm going to freshen up a bit," she added over her shoulder. "Answer the door if I'm not ready, and let Dwayne in, would you?"

"Sure, Mom." Freshen up. Dwayne. That sounded good. And that made Kim think of music. She rushed to put a tape called *Moon Silver* on the tape deck in the living room. And what about food? She hurried to the kitchen and got out the cheese board and cheese. She set out two glasses for cool drinks.

Just as she finished, her mother came back down the hall. Kim blinked her eyes in disappointment. Her mother hadn't changed her clothes or anything. She was wearing the same old office dress.

Suddenly, the doorbell rang. Kim hurried back to the living room in time to see her mother opening the front door, ushering someone in, then turning toward Kim.

"This is my daughter, Kim," she was saying. "Kim, this is Mr. Higby."

Kim looked toward him and saw with sudden sadness that Dwayne from the office had an awfully large stomach and was very old. Why, he might die soon! He might not have time to be her father.

"How do you do, young lady?" he said.

"How do you do?" Kim answered.

Maybe he was just tired. Maybe he looked older than he really was, she told herself.

"Kim." There was a tiny frown on her mother's face. "Could you turn off that music, please?" Kim felt a surge of disappointment and noticed, too, that there was no drift of Spring Passion perfume from her mother. "And when Randy comes home, could you please keep him out in the yard?"

Kim's heart lifted again. Her mother was setting things up right after all. Maybe Dwayne was hard of hearing. Maybe that's why she didn't want the music.

"Yes, Mom. Good-bye, Mr. Higby." She smiled politely. It was important that he like her, too. She went out front then to sit on the front steps and watch for Randy. The nursery school van would be along pretty soon. And while she waited, maybe Mike would come by on his bike. How could she get him to stop and talk? Maybe she could ask him about the career contest. She glanced nervously toward the Ridleys' house next door and hoped that Lorraine wouldn't show up. Lorraine

16

seemed to have a way of appearing whenever Kim was outside.

Out at the curb, Dwayne's car was parked — a gray Alfa Romeo — and from inside the house came hardly any sounds at all. If she listened hard, she could barely hear Dwayne's voice speaking in a slow way. It didn't sound like much fun, not like her dad's loud, happy laugh.

She leaned forward to peer up Palm Street, lined with stucco houses and small trees, and saw the van coming at last. She jumped up and ran out to the curb to meet it. She'd have to figure out a way to keep Randy outside. If only she'd thought about it, she could've brought out his favorite toy, a toy stove. He loved to pretend to cook on it.

The van pulled up in front of Dwayne's car and the side door slid open. "Hi, Randy," Kim called, hurrying over to him.

Randy, a backpack slung over his shoulders, his brown hair all mussed up, hopped out of the van.

"You want to play a game, Randy?" Kim asked quickly.

"Isn't Mom home?" Already he looked suspicious. "I wanna go inside and see Mom." Randy pushed out his lower lip.

"Wait, Randy. Let's do something fun. Mom asked me to keep you outside. A man is in there. Dwayne, from the office."

Randy's round face looked unimpressed. Kim wondered sometimes if Randy remembered ever having a dad.

"Well, I don't care." Randy turned toward the front door.

"No, Randy." Kim ran after him. "Listen." She tried to think how to explain it to him. "Mom might start dating this man, you see. Then, who knows? Maybe she might get married again. Then we'd have another dad. And guess what? You could probably have a dog, because Mom might be home more of the time."

Kim knew that was what Randy wanted right now, but their mom had said no to the idea, since she'd started working full-time.

Randy paused and looked up at her. "Oh, okay. I don't care about the dad part, but I'll take the dog."

"Right. So look, for right now, do you want to do some stunts, somersaults or something?"

"Sure." He got a gleam in his eyes. "Stand on your head."

Kim groaned. "Well, okay." At least she was wearing jeans. She kneeled on the lawn, put her head down on the ground, and tried to raise her legs in the air. She was just about doing it, too, waving her legs wildly to keep her balance.

Suddenly she heard a voice call out from the street, "Hey, terrific."

She tumbled over quickly and sat up. Mike Martines!

He was pedaling up to her house on his bike. He stopped and put his feet down on the pavement and grinned at her. Why did he have to catch her upside down with her feet in the air?

She stood up, brushing off her jeans. "Hi," she said. "I was just doing some stunts for my brother." Her face must be totally bright red and her hair all a mess. She tried to smooth it into place.

Just at that moment, the Ridley car came down the street and pulled into their driveway. Lorraine was peering out the window and laughing.

"Here come your new neighbors," Mike said cheerfully.

"I know," Kim said, and wondered how he felt about Lorraine.

The car doors opened and Lorraine and her parents got out. Mr. Ridley, newspaper under his arm, headed for their house, but Mrs. Ridley and Lorraine came round the side of the car and into Kim's yard.

"Some show you're putting on," Lorraine called out, a big grin still on her face.

"Hello, Kim," Mrs. Ridley said. "Is your mother home from work yet? Or are you here by yourselves?" Mrs. Ridley's voice was commanding, as if she was used to getting answers. Kim felt as if

Mrs. Ridley was checking up on them. "No, I mean, yes, Mom's home."

"She's got a man in there, so we have to stay outside," Randy piped up.

"Oh, I see." Mrs. Ridley's thin, plucked eyebrows rose high on her forehead, and Lorraine smiled knowingly. Kim wanted to say, "Don't look that way, there's nothing wrong with my mom having a visitor."

To Kim's disappointment, Mike said then, "I gotta go," and slid back onto his bike and pedaled off.

" 'Bye, Mike," Kim managed to say.

"Stop by again," Lorraine called out loudly.

But then her mother said, "Come, Lorraine, time to start supper. Say hello to your mother, Kim, and be sure to tell her to let me know if she ever needs any assistance. When she gets through with her visitor, that is."

They turned to leave, Lorraine saying something to her mother about wanting to talk to her dad before dinner. Lucky Lorraine, thought Kim, to have a dad.

Kim watched the two of them, mother and daughter, as they walked with very straight backs across the lawn, both of them tall, blonde, and acting so sure of themselves.

"Randy," Kim said as the Ridleys went in their house, "you don't have to tell them everything."

"What'd I say?" Randy kicked moodily at the dirt. "I want to go inside and play with my stove."

Kim sighed and looked up the street for a minute. One of the neighbors, Mr. Ferraro, was out front throwing a ball back and forth with his son, Tony.

She turned to Randy. "Look, how about I get the soccer ball out of the garage and we'll play for a while?" Sometimes she did get tired of kicking this ball around with Randy. If only he had a dad!

4.
Like Real Hair

"A nd there I was, standing on my head," Kim exclaimed the next afternoon to Angie. They were walking down Parkway Drive on their way to school, peering in the shop windows.

"Well, that's not so bad," Angie said.

Kim paused to peer into a shoe-shop window, reliving her disappointment of yesterday. Her mom hadn't used the cheese or passed out any refreshments at all. She'd just taken notes in her black notebook. Then last night she'd sat at her desk, typing away. Dwayne, it turned out, had made a very large sale and needed her mother to help his secretary work on the contract.

"What are you doing for your career report?" Angie asked, interrupting Kim's thoughts.

"I'm trying to think of something different and exciting," Kim said. "Have you decided yet?" All the sixth-grade classes were doing career reports.

They started to walk again. "Yes. I'm going to write about a police officer, and my mom's going to take me to visit the police station. Won't that be terrific?" Angie's whole face lit up.

"That'll be great, Angie," Kim agreed. But Kim felt a stab of sadness. If only she could think of something good, too! But nothing seemed that terrific . . . not teacher, nurse, doctor, lawyer, sales clerk, certainly not office worker, like her mom. She wanted to find something special and unusual.

They walked on, continuing to peer into the store windows. At the drugstore they paused to admire a display of some huge, curling eyelashes and some long, pointed fake fingernails that looked almost dangerous. Then behind them were . . . Kim gasped. Wigs! Blonde, red-haired, and brown, on plastic heads! "Be Beautiful," a sign read. "Final close-out sale."

"Angie." She clutched her friend's arm. "Look at those wigs, would you?"

"Yeah, pretty, aren't they?"

"Angie, don't you see? That's what I ought to do, get one for my mom."

"Kim." Angie rolled her dark eyes in amazement. "What an idea." She bent toward the glass window and so did Kim.

"See that blonde one?" Kim pointed excitedly. "Wouldn't that look good on my mom?"

"I guess." Angie looked a little doubtful. "Why don't you tell her about it?"

Kim shook her head. "I know she wouldn't do it. She'd say it costs too much. Our budget is really tight these days."

"I wonder what it does cost," Angie said.

"Let's see." Kim bent her head sideways, trying to read the price tag. "Why, look!" she exclaimed. "They're on close-out sale, only four ninety-nine — " She broke off as a wonderful idea suddenly came to her. "Angie, I know what. I could give one to Mom for an early birthday present. I think I'll just go right in there and buy one."

Angie looked admiring. "Well, why not? It's such a bargain. But where will you get the money?"

Kim started for the door. "No problem, I have some with me. It's for my lunches, but I could pack my lunches instead. Come on with me, Angie."

They hurried into the lighted interior of the drugstore, the shelves lined with bottles and cartons of medicine, a counter filled with cosmetics. Kim and Angie paused in front of it.

"Hi," Kim said to the salesgirl standing there. "Could I see that wig in the window? The blonde one?"

"Sure thing." The salesgirl's own hair was a large, kinky blonde mass that looked sort of like a wig, too. She went over to the window and brought back the wig to Kim. "It's a super nice one," she said, handing it to Kim.

Kim took it and almost said ouch. It was so scratchy. It felt like the scouring pads she scrubbed the pans with.

"I guess the way it feels doesn't matter, does it?" she asked. She held it out at arm's length. "It's great, don't you think, Angie?"

"It sure is," Angie agreed loyally. "Great."

"Well, you know what they say." The salesgirl fluffed her hair. "Blondes have more fun." She grinned at them. "Here," she added, leading them over to a mirror. "Come try it on."

Kim followed her to the mirror and pulled on the wig without bothering to tuck her own hair up under it. She raised her eyebrows, tilting her head from side to side.

"Would this be good on my mom?" she wondered aloud. She peered at herself and tried to picture her mother's face under that blonde crown, but it was hard to get past her own questioning face and puzzled blue eyes.

"Sure," Angie said. "It'd look great on your mother, Kim. I think she'd love it."

Suddenly, there was loud laughter behind them, and a voice said, "Well, what do you think you're doing?"

Kim turned, startled. Lorraine was just coming

in the door. Kim felt herself getting hot with embarrassment, and to her disgust, she saw her own face in the mirror, turning pink. Before she could think of what to say, Lorraine added, coolly, "Don't you know it's not a hat? You're supposed to stick your hair under it."

"I know that." Kim was determined to be equally cool. "I was in a hurry to try it on, that's all." She wished Lorraine would leave.

Lorraine came over and circled. "Well, that's some wig," she pronounced in a superior voice. "What's it for? Halloween?"

"Of course not," Kim said shortly. "Lots of people wear wigs."

"Yeah," Angie agreed.

Lorraine shrugged. "Well, okay. I was just asking." She leaned against the glass case. "Have you two picked your careers yet for the contest? I'm doing a social worker, like my mom. Sometimes she lets me read her reports and stuff."

Kim heard this with a sinking heart. It sounded great.

"I'm doing a policewoman," Angie spoke up.

"I haven't decided yet," Kim admitted.

Lorraine straightened up. "Well, I have to go. My dad's coming home early tonight to take me to the mall. He's usually so busy. He's a very important consultant, you know."

Lucky Lorraine, Kim couldn't help thinking

again, always doing things with her dad. Just at that moment she happened to glance past Lorraine to the windows. There were a couple of boys lurking outside, peering in and laughing.

"What are they laughing at?" Kim exclaimed. But now the boys ducked out of sight. "I think one of them was Mike."

Lorraine whirled around. "Where? Where? Well, I guess I have to go. My dad doesn't like to be kept waiting."

She rushed out the door, slamming it after her. It was very quiet in the drugstore. In the back somewhere, a phone rang, and the white-coated pharmacist began to talk into it. Kim smiled at Angie. "I don't really think Mike was out there."

Angie laughed. "Guess you got rid of her." Angie sounded pleased. "She should know you've already got friends."

Kim heard the note of worry in Angela's voice. "That's the truth." She smiled at Angela, then turned to look at herself in the mirror again. "I still think this is a nice wig."

"It is. Forget Lorraine," Angie said.

"Never mind your friend," the salesgirl agreed. "That wig would look real good on your mom, for sure."

Kim looked back in the mirror. She tilted her head a few more times. "Yes, I think you're right. I'll take it," she decided.

A few minutes later, Kim and Angie were out on the street, Kim clutching the wig box in her arms.

"Oh, Angie, don't you think Mom will love this?" She half closed her eyes. "I wonder what it'll look like on her." She tried to visualize it, the blonde taking the place of her mom's brown hair, and beneath it, the sad face, the eyes that never seemed to light up anymore. But maybe now, now they would. They'd have to when she saw this wonderful wig.

5.
It's Not a Cat

Kim hurried down Palm Street. She didn't like this time of day very much, coming home to an empty house. True, Mrs. Greenberg was usually watching out her window about this time, with her cat, Peter, sitting on the sill beside her like a white statue. But back in the old days, her mom would've been at home taking care of Randy and cooking dinner. Now Kim had to help with all that, too.

Well, today she had something really exciting to think about while she worked. She waved to Mrs. Greenberg as she hurried up the walk, then pulled out her door key from her shoulder bag and unlocked the front door. Inside, she turned on music good and loud, and rushed to her room to start wrapping the wig box.

What would her mom say when she opened it? Maybe she'd smile and say, "Well, let's have a barbecue this weekend, the way we used to."

And Kim would ask, "How about that new family up the street, Mike and his parents?" It *would* be like the old days, when there were kids running through the house and grown-ups out back, laughing and cooking chicken and hamburgers.

Kim tried to make dinner extra good that evening. Her mom had left her a list of things to do, as usual. Kim washed the lettuce three times so there wouldn't be any grit in it, and was careful to pick the stems off the cherry tomatoes.

After she set the table, she went out into the backyard and found a few yellow leaves and put them in a vase on the kitchen table.

When her mom saw them that evening, she smiled. "How pretty. Thanks, dear."

Kim decided to wait until dinner was over before presenting the wig to her. No use taking a chance. Something might get spilled or dripped onto it. Randy often knocked things over and made a mess.

Kim waited impatiently while they ate. She tried to think about other things. She talked about school and the career reports. "Angie's going to write about being a policewoman. Sara hasn't decided."

"What are you planning, Kim?"

Kim hoped her mom wouldn't suggest she do a secretary. But she didn't want to tell her that and maybe hurt her feelings. "I haven't decided yet, Mom," she said, taking a bite of the pasta her mother had fixed. "I wish I could think of something really good."

"I'm going to be a real cook when I grow up." Randy smashed his pasta, sending pieces flying. "People will go crazy for my food."

Kim ignored Randy and went on talking. "Lorraine is going to do a social worker, like her mom. She's always bragging about her mother's job. Her dad's, too." Kim suddenly wished she hadn't said that. She never boasted about her own mom's job. And it was probably just as hard and just as good as anything Lorraine's mom did. She said quickly, "What's a consultant, Mom? That's what Lorraine's dad is."

"Well, a consultant advises and helps." Mrs. Conway frowned, looking thoughtful. "But I don't know what Mr. Ridley's field is."

At last, dinner was over. While her mother was still sitting at the kitchen table, sipping her coffee, Kim hurried to her room for the gift-wrapped box. So Lorraine had laughed at it. Who cared?

"Mom," she said, returning to the table. "Could I give you a birthday present early? I know it's not till next month, but I saw this today." She handed her mother the box. If only her mom would like it!

"What is it? A present? What is it?" Randy came running back to the table from his little stove, where he'd been stirring leftover pasta in a pan.

"Why, Kim." Surprise crossed her mom's thin face. "But shouldn't I wait until my birthday?"

"No, Mom. Please open it now. I saw it, and it was such a good bargain."

Her mother started to pull off the paper, a little frown creasing her forehead. "I hope you haven't spent a lot of money on me."

"No, really, I didn't."

Mom lifted the lid and sat for a minute, looking into the box.

"What's in there?" Randy grabbed the edge of the box and peered inside. "What's that? A cat?" He stuck his hand in to touch it.

"Ow-w-w! It pricked me."

"Randy, be quiet." Kim pulled him back. She should never have given this to her mom while he was around. "Let Mom open her present."

Mrs. Conway lifted the wig out of the box. "Oh, Kim." She was quiet for a moment. "That's, uh, so thoughtful of you, darling." Her voice sounded a little strangled, but she leaned over and kissed Kim on the cheek and hugged her tight for a minute. "My nice Kim, what a wonderful daughter." Then she looked at the wig again. "But wigs are awfully expensive, aren't they?"

"No, no, Mom. It wasn't much."

But her mother was holding it up on her hand, looking worried. "Maybe you'd better tell me what it cost, Kim. I realize it is a gift, but I'd feel better if I knew."

"It was only four ninety-nine. I got it on a *big* close-out sale." Now Mom could stop worrying, though in a way, Kim wished she could say it had cost more.

"Well, that *is* a good price," Mrs. Conway said in a kind of funny way. She had a little smile on her face.

"I used my lunch money, Mom," Kim went on eagerly. "But I'll take my lunch for a while to make up for it. It'll taste better than that mystery food at school, anyway."

"Well, I like you to have a hot lunch, but thanks, dear. That's quite a surprise to have an early birthday present." Mrs. Conway leaned over and gave Kim another hug.

"Try it on, Mom." Kim could hardly wait to see what it looked like.

Mrs. Conway straightened up and pulled the wig on her head and tucked her own brown hair under it. Now she was smiling again. She looked at Kim and Randy. "How do I look, kids?"

"Funny." Randy screwed up his face horribly. "You don't look like my mom."

"Good, Mom. Really pretty." Kim glowered at Randy. She really should have given it to her mom when Randy wasn't around. He'd give her the wrong idea, for sure, though in a way, she had to agree with him. Her mom did look different. But that was the point, wasn't it, to change yourself?

"Go look in the mirror." Kim jumped up and took the box off her mother's lap.

Mrs. Conway got up and went out to the hall, Kim following her. She peered in the mirror over the hall stand. She was quiet for a moment. "I do look different, don't I?" She turned to Kim. "Thanks again, honey. I'll save it for special occasions."

But when would that be, Kim wondered. Her mother went down the hall to her room then, calling to Randy to come for his bath. It was just her ordinary voice again, as if she'd forgotten all about the wig.

"Yay-y-y!" Randy went racing after her. He liked to pretend he was going swimming when he took a bath, and he splashed a lot of water around, too.

But as Kim started back to the kitchen, she noticed her mother had paused in the doorway of her bedroom. She looked sad standing there. Was she gazing at the big framed photograph of Kim's dad on her bureau, wishing she could bring him back? But what was the use of that? Kim wanted to call out to her mother, "He's gone now. Gone for good. Remember what Aunt Ruth used to say about letting go of the past?"

Kim returned to the kitchen, picked up the dirty dishes, and slid them under the hot water faucet. She had hoped her mom would start wearing the wig right away, tomorrow even, to the office. She wished her mom had said something like, "Well, now I think I'll go out more, maybe start dating." But she hadn't said anything like that.

As the steam rose up into Kim's face, she blinked her eyes against the tears that wanted to come. The wig hadn't helped at all. Kim hunched over the kitchen sink, trying to get rid of a feeling of disappointment. Maybe she could help her mom find a special occasion soon, when she could wear it.

6.
Great Ideas

Before classes the next morning, Kim hurried across the playground, looking for Angie and Sara. They were kicking a ball back and forth with some other girls, but when they saw Kim, they ran over to her.

"Kim, how was it?" Angie came panting up to her, brushing her dark, fuzzy hair out of her face. "Did she like the wig? I told Sara about it."

"Yes, how was it?" Her two friends looked at her eagerly, and Kim wished she had better news.

"I guess she liked it. She said she'd save it for some special time. Trouble is," Kim frowned, looking off across the playground, "she doesn't really have any."

"It's a shame. My mom says it must be really tough for your mom," Angie said sympathetically.

"Yes," Sara agreed. "She should get out more." She snapped her fingers suddenly, pink polish gleaming on her fingernails in the sunlight. "I've got an idea. Why don't you come over some day?

We could look in the *Singles* magazine my mom has. We might get some great ideas."

"Sara, terrific. I'd love to." Kim felt a sudden burst of hope. Looking at *Singles* magazine might be just the thing. Now, if only she could come up with a good idea for her career report, too.

That night, when she settled down to work on her report, Kim started to thumb through the newspaper, looking for suggestions. She paused to read a cartoon, when she noticed an article about a veterinary school back in the Midwest. There were pictures of students walking across campus. Why, some of them looked fairly old, as old as her mom. And quite a few were men!

Kim hunched over the paper and read all about it. It sounded like a great kind of a school. When she finished, she threw the paper down in excitement. She began to get ready for bed, thinking hard about what she'd just read. There must be a vet school around here somewhere. And there must be some men there who weren't married or who weren't as old as Dwayne and didn't have such big stomachs. Now she knew what her mom ought to do, and what career she'd choose for her project. What a great idea it was, too. Almost in a trance, Kim pulled back her tufted quilt, slipped in under the covers, and snapped out the light.

She lay in her bed, gazing out her window at the streetlight outside, thinking about what might happen. Her mom would meet someone really nice there and after a while they'd get married. They'd be like a real family again, with a mom and a dad, not with this emptiness in their house anymore. A feeling of hope flooded through Kim's mind as she gazed at the yellow glow of the streetlight, falling through the window. It looked almost like soft moonlight. Then her eyelids were closing, and she couldn't stay awake any longer.

At breakfast the next morning Kim said, "Mom, did you ever think of going back to school?"

"School?" Randy echoed. "Kids go to school, not moms." He banged his spoon loudly on the table.

"Randy-y-y." Kim frowned at him. He was such a dope, no help at all. Besides, if he knew it was a school about cats and dogs, he'd want to go there himself.

"What do you think, Mom?" Kim persisted. "You could use the insurance money from the accident." For a long time, Kim had tried never to mention the car crash, as if by doing that it meant it hadn't happened. When she'd make a new friend, she'd avoid saying anything at all about her dad.

Her mom pushed her hair off her forehead and frowned a little. "Well, we need to save the money, Kim. We have to eat and make payments on the house and buy clothes and all that."

"But maybe doing something else would be better. You know, more fun." Kim didn't dare mention meeting men at veterinarian school. It would just annoy her mom.

"Kim, I have the skills to be a secretary. Of course, if I'd known we'd lose Dad, I might've majored in something more practical in college than history." Mrs. Conway let out a sigh and began to slice bananas over a bowl of cereal for Randy. "Sure, there are other things I might be doing, but it would be hard to give up this good job. So there's no use thinking about anything else, Kim."

But Kim didn't see how she could stop thinking about it. It seemed like such a fabulous idea. Going to vet school could solve everything, and it was much more exciting than the wig. No way was she going to give up this idea. When her mom thought about it some more, she'd probably change her mind.

7.
Choosing

Kim couldn't wait to report her career idea to Mr. Chang that day. Finally, during last period, he began talking about the projects.

"Boys and girls, I hope you've been thinking seriously about careers. Remember, when you're older you'll have to make important decisions about what kind of work you'll do." His dark eyes looked at them earnestly. "Some day, you'll be in charge of this world, and it'll be up to you to run things. So I hope you give your future a lot of thought. Now, have you all selected your subjects? A few of you have already told me your choices."

Kim shot her hand into the air. When Mr. Chang nodded at her, she said, "I'd like to sign up for veterinarian work, Mr. Chang."

"Good, good, Kim." He looked approving, she thought, as he wrote it down. Then he read aloud the list of occupations the others had already signed up for. When he read that Lorraine had picked social work, to help people with their problems, Kim was afraid he looked even more approving.

Kim sent a swift glance toward Sara. Was Lorraine going to beat them?

Mr. Chang wrote down some of the other students' choices and then he said, "Who has parents in these occupations? Perhaps they'd be willing to be interviewed by our students."

Lorraine raised her hand confidently. "My mother would. She's a social worker, and she helps a lot of families in trouble, like single parents and kids on their own." She pressed her lips together in a self-important way.

A boy named Bill Slotsky began to tell how his mother was a helicopter mechanic, and she'd be willing to be interviewed. Heather said her mother stayed home to raise three children, and she thought that was a good career, too. Sara said her mother was a hostess in a restaurant and met a lot of wonderful people and would love to talk about it. Then something really amazing happened. Mike raised his hand and said, "I've signed up for a park ranger myself, but both my mom and dad are veterinarians. They've opened The Small Pet Clinic here in town." Mike threw a quick glance toward Kim.

Veterinarians? Kim stared at Mike. His mother and father? Why, how fantastic! What luck! What

41

an astounding coincidence! Then a thought exploded in her mind, like a rocket going off in space. She could go talk to his parents at their clinic . . . if they'd let her. She could find out a whole lot that way. When her report was finished, she'd ask her mom to read it, and when her mom found out Mike's mom was a vet, too, that might really help make her want to go to vet school. Also, it would be a great report, maybe even better than Lorraine's. A last happy thought crossed her mind. Maybe Mike would come to the clinic that day, too.

She looked over her shoulder at Sara, but Sara was listening raptly to a boy who was explaining that his dad was an actor on a daytime TV program, one of the "soaps," called *Time of Our Lives.*

Kim could feel the excitement welling up inside her. Her report would be so good she'd be one of the winners and have her picture in the paper, and her mom would be really impressed. Kim wished Sara would look her way so she could signal her excitement.

But now the discussion seemed to be ending, and then Lorraine had her hand up again. "Mr. Chang, can we change our minds and pick another career?" Kim's heart took a low dive.

But Mr. Chang could be firm. "We can't all start

changing around. You already have a very good idea, Lorraine."

Lorraine looked cross. Kim's heart lifted up again. Only she would get to go to Mike's clinic. Of course, she was doing this for her mom, but see how well it was working out for her, too!

Out in the hallway after class, she and Sara hurried toward each other.

"That was close." Sara grinned. "You were really smart, Kim, to pick being a vet."

"Well, of course I didn't know both of Mike's parents were vets," Kim said modestly. "Isn't that just great?"

"You bet!" Sara looked impressed. "No wonder Lorraine wanted to get in on your idea."

"I know, I know," Kim agreed. They were standing there giggling about it, when suddenly Kim glanced up and saw Lorraine coming toward them.

"Uh, hi," Lorraine said. "So you're going to interview Mike's parents?"

"I hope so. If they agree," Kim said.

"And you're going to their clinic?"

Kim could see the longing on Lorraine's face. "If they'll let me." Kim glanced toward Sara. Lorraine was trying to get in on this part, too. If she came, she'd do all the talking and try to take over.

Just then, Mike came up behind Lorraine. "Hi."

He grinned. "So you want to know about vets, huh? Want me to ask my dad and mom if you can come see their clinic?"

"Oh, yes, would you? That'd be so great, Mike. Could I interview one of them? Are they both called Dr. Martines?"

"Well, my mom's name is Dr. Lee Martines, and my father's name is Dr. John Martines. But they both go by Dr. Martines. I'll ask them tonight if you can come. How about tomorrow?"

"Terrific." Kim smiled at him joyfully.

"No problem." Mike snapped his fingers, then raced off down the hall after some boys.

Kim took a deep breath. She wished he'd be there, too. But would he? And would his parents really say yes?

"That sounds like fun," Lorraine said loudly. "I'd like to see that pet clinic."

Just then, Kim spotted Angie in the crowd up ahead. "Angie," she called. "Come on, Sara," she said over her shoulder. They rushed off down the hall to tell Angie the news. Besides, Kim was eager to get away from Lorraine.

8.
Stop That Dog

Kim was so excited the next day she could hardly wait for school to end so she could go visit The Small Pet Clinic. Mike had come up to her in the hall first thing that morning and said his mom would be at the clinic today and would be glad to have Kim visit. Then he rushed off down the hall. She didn't even get to thank him. She wished she could've found out if he was coming, too, but she never had a chance to talk to him again that whole day.

Lorraine wanted to talk to her, though, Kim could tell, and she could just guess what it was about. So every time she saw Lorraine headed her way, Kim hurried off. Once she ran to kick a ball across the playground to Sara, once to join some other girls skipping rope. And at lunchtime, Kim asked Sara and Angie to sit on the other side of the cafeteria with her, far away from Lorraine. Unfortunately, she was far away from Mike, too.

"Mike will probably be at the clinic," Angie consoled her. "Don't worry. Besides, think of all the great dogs and cats you're going to see."

"I know." Kim looked off across the cafeteria and tried to think about cats and dogs. Now Lorraine had jumped up from her place and was talking to Mike and some others over by the trash can. Was she asking if she could come, too? If only Lorraine hadn't moved onto her street and into her life!

That afternoon, as Kim set off, she began to have other worries, too. Would she be able to ask the right questions? Would Dr. Lee Martines really want to talk to her?

Kim had told her mom all about it this morning, mentioning several times that both Mike's mom and dad were veterinarians.

"Really?" Mrs. Conway had looked impressed. "That sounds like a very good project, dear."

Kim wanted to tell her just how really good it was — she was bursting to, in fact. But not yet, she decided. It'd be better to find out more about vet school before she suggested it to her mom. So Kim had just smiled and said, "I think it will make a great report." Then she said again, "Isn't it terrific that Mike's mom is a vet, too?"

So now she was hurrying down Marino Street, then turning onto Parkway Drive, where all the shops and gas stations and markets were. She walked more slowly, thinking of the questions she should ask and feeling somewhat nervous.

But when she finally came to The Small Pet Clinic and pushed open the door, she began to feel excited again. There in the waiting room a woman sat holding a cage with a gorgeous tawny cat inside. Across from her a white-haired man had the cutest black Scottie on a leash. What a fun job it would be for her mom, and what a great report it was going to be. Kim walked over to a counter where a freckle-faced woman stood, talking into the phone. While Kim waited, her hopes rose. When the secretary finished talking, she turned to Kim. "Yes? May I help you?"

"Hi," Kim said, suddenly wishing the man and woman weren't watching and listening. "My name is Kim Conway, and I've come to interview — "

"Oh, sure, hon. Doctor's expecting you. Come right this way." With a fleeting glance over her shoulder, hoping she'd see Mike come in the door, Kim followed the secretary. They went down a long hall. A sharp smell of disinfectant floated on the air, and from the back came the steady yip of a dog. At the end of the hall, the woman led Kim into a small office.

"Just have a seat here," she said, and turned and left. Kim sat down on a leather couch and eyed the small room. The walls were covered with framed diplomas and certificates. The large desk had a row of thick volumes on it. Kim was picturing her mother sitting there and reading them, when Dr. Lee Martinos walked into the room.

"Hello, Kim. Glad to see you." She was short and dark-haired, and to Kim's relief, she was smiling. "Mike told me you want to know about our work here." She held out a small hand and gave Kim a firm handshake. Then she sat down behind the desk.

"Oh, yes, Dr. Martines. Thank you for letting me come." Right away Kim began to relax. Dr. Lee Martines didn't mind the visit, Kim could tell. "I'd like to do my report about veterinarians." She thought of the article in the paper. Why not get right to the point. "I was wondering how you go about applying to veterinarian school. Is it very hard to get in?"

"Yes, it's very competitive." Dr. Martines frowned a little. "There aren't very many schools of veterinary medicine, you see. So in order to get in, you need to have good grades. It also helps if you like the life sciences and if you've had some experience with animals, too."

Kim was sure her mom had done well in school and had liked it. She'd also had a dog for many years when she was a girl. "What's vet school like?" Kim asked, wondering just how her mother might fit in.

Dr. Martines laughed a little. "Hectic, really fast-paced. There is so much to study. We had to learn about many kinds of species — cows and farm animals for one — then cats and dogs, also exotic birds and reptiles. It's a heavy schedule."

"Is there any time for, uh, fun, seeing friends and all that?"

"Oh, yes. We had some parties. That's where I met Mike's dad, in fact."

"Really?" Kim was ecstatic. "Is there a school near here?"

"Well, the only one is the state university. That's not so close."

Kim's hopes sagged, and maybe her disappointment showed because Dr. Lee Martines added, "There are some nearby schools, like Southwest College, where courses are given that would help you prepare. Those are science courses in things like biology and zoology, embryology, and so on. You can take them before going on to the university. That's just what I did."

Kim's hopes soared. "How do you sign up for them?"

"Well, let's see. I could get you a catalog for Southwest College and mail it to you. You can see what the pre-vet courses are like."

"Oh, could you? Thank you." Kim clasped her hands eagerly.

Dr. Martines smiled at Kim. "I'm glad you're so interested in animal care. Now, what else do you need to know?"

Kim frowned and looked around the little office. "What's it like here every day? What do you do exactly?"

Dr. Lee Martines began to talk about giving immunization injections and about caring for animals hurt in accidents. "And there're other kinds of things. Just now I treated a Labrador retriever for some ear problems and showed his owner how to put drops in his dog's ears. Earlier, I stitched up a cut in a collie's leg."

Kim pulled out a notebook and wrote fast, feeling elated. What a report this was going to be! Why, she was sure to be one of the winners. And wouldn't her mother love the whole idea of going to vet school — though when Dr. Martines mentioned that tomorrow she was doing surgery and would be removing a parrot's eye, Kim had a few qualms. Would her mom like that part?

Suddenly the door opened and Mike stood in the doorway. "Hi," he said. How cute he looked with his dark curly hair and dark eyes. Now Kim knew this was a terrific day, for sure.

"Hello, Mike. I'm glad you're here." His mother rose to her feet. "Could you take Kim in the back and show her around? I must get back to work."

"Sure, Mom. Anything you want us to do? Should we walk any dogs or anything?"

"I could help," Kim exclaimed. She loved the idea of walking dogs with Mike.

Dr. Lee Martines looked pleased. "Well, I am short-handed today. Our assistant couldn't come. We do have a standard poodle who got very muddy out in the country. His owner brought him in for a bath. It's a warm day. You could wash him out back."

"We could handle that." Mike poked his thumbs in his belt and grinned at Kim. "Couldn't we, Kim?"

"Oh, yes, yes," Kim exclaimed. Washing a darling poodle, why not? She couldn't think of anything more fun in this world right now than washing a dog with Mike.

She couldn't stop smiling as she followed Mike out to the hall and on to the back of the clinic. This was going to be fabulous. If her mom really did become a vet, Kim decided, she'd come help her every day after school.

They went into a room lined with cages, where dogs moved restlessly behind bars, and cats glared indignantly. The air was thick with animal smells. Mike led her out the rear door. To Kim's surprise, the standard poodle turned out to be a big dog with lots of thick curly white hair. He was in a small fenced area behind the clinic and came running eagerly up to them.

"Oh, he's nice," Kim exclaimed, patting his curly hair. She looked at the name tag fastened to his collar. "His name's Jasper. Hi, Jasper."

"Yeah, he looks okay, doesn't he? We'll wash him out here," Mike added, and he brought out a big tub and a hose with a sprayer attached. In a few minutes they had coaxed Jasper into the tub and began to rub a soapy solution all over his fur. "This stuff will get rid of fleas and ticks, too. Then after we do this, we'll spray him off. He won't like that part, I'm afraid," Mike said.

But at least Jasper didn't mind so far, and Kim thought how great this was. She gave the dog a few loving pats. "This is really nice of you, Mike, and your mom, to let me come here." She smiled at him.

"Yeah, it's okay, isn't it?" And as they washed the dog, sometimes their soapy hands bumped against each other, and Kim didn't mind that, either.

"Now we'll rinse him off," Mike said after a few minutes. "I'll go turn on the water." He stepped inside to the back room for a minute. "It's warm, you see," he explained, coming back outside.

But at the sound of the rushing water, Jasper began to shiver. "Uh-oh, he's not going to like this!" Kim exclaimed.

Just then, a truck stopped in the alley behind the fenced area. A delivery man leaped out of the truck, carrying a big load of boxes, and came over to the gate. "Hi, there," he said.

"Aaarf!" Jasper barked. With that, he bounded

forward, knocked the man down, spilled his boxes everywhere, and raced off through the gate.

"Hey, Jasper, come back here!" Mike bellowed, sprinting after him.

"Jasper!" Kim shouted, and raced after both of them.

But Jasper was free now, and he ran out into the alley and darted around the corner of the building.

"I'll go this way," Mike yelled to Kim. "You go the other way."

Kim raced off around the other side of the clinic and out onto Parkway Drive, where people were walking along the sidewalk. Just then, Jasper came streaking toward her through the crowd. Kim leaped toward him. He swerved away from her and ran on. But a few yards away he stopped for a minute and shook himself hard, sending a soapy spray flying all over three ladies.

"Stop! Stop that dog!" the ladies shrieked.

Kim flew after him and grabbed him, but his fur was so wet and slippery he darted right out from under her hands. Kim started to run, but she skidded wildly on the wet pavement and fell down on her hands and knees. And as she looked up, she couldn't believe her eyes. A whole crowd of people stood there laughing at her, and one of them was Lorraine.

9.
Filling Out the Form

Kim tried to think about the report she was writing. Forget about the disaster at The Small Pet Clinic, she told herself. Forget about how all those people laughed at her, especially dumb old Lorraine. Mike had run on ahead and finally caught that big, wet, escaping Jasper.

Now if only the catalog to Southwest College would come from Dr. Martines. It was sure to make a great report, and wasn't her mom going to love the whole idea?

That evening, Kim heard her mom talking on the phone to her friend Jan. "Yes, Jan, it's really hard, isn't it?" she heard her mom say. Jan was in the French Club her mother belonged to, and every few weeks the club members met and practiced speaking French. "Yes, I know, it's really something the way the bills pile up," Mrs. Conway went on. "You just have to watch the budget every minute, don't you?" Jan had three children to raise, and she was a single parent, too.

A little later, when Kim went into her mom's room, Mrs. Conway was hunched over her desk, her checkbook open, a stack of bills beside her. Kim longed to tell her about her secret plan. She wanted to rush over to her and say, "Listen, Mom, I've got this great idea. You'd meet new people, new men, start dating, get married again. We'd have a dad to help us. Things would be the way they used to be."

But for now, all she said was, "Mom, want me to fix you a cup of tea?"

Her mother looked up with a tired smile. "Sure, dear. That'd be nice."

Kim decided she'd wait a little longer until the catalog came.

Each day she looked eagerly through the mail. One afternoon, when she came home, there it was, a big brown envelope addressed to her. Kim ripped it open, and inside was the Southwest catalog, along with an application form. Kim studied it with mounting excitement. Why not fill out the application for her mother and save her all that trouble?

Kim rushed to the phone and dialed Angie. "Angie, guess what? It came, the stuff about the vet school and the application. I've got the greatest idea. I'm going to fill it out for Mom. Do you think you could come over and help me with it? Right away?" She glanced at the clock. It was late because she'd stopped at the library on the way home to do some reading for her report.

"Sure, Kim. I'd like to." Angie was always happy to get away from her three brothers.

After Kim hung up, she hurried to her mother's room and began to hunt through her desk. It had a lot of little drawers and compartments, but Kim knew her mom kept important papers in a large manila folder.

Finally, Kim found it. But before opening it, she went over to her dad's silver-framed picture on the bureau. "Dad, you'd think this was a good idea, wouldn't you? Mom's so sad and lonesome, and she works so hard." Of course, they'd never talked about what to do if he died, never expected such a thing to happen. She stared into his still face, looking out at her forever now with that same expression, his eyes serious behind his glasses. But how had he looked other times? How had his voice sounded? It was getting harder and harder to remember him as the days and weeks rolled by. The thought made Kim sad.

She hurried back to her mom's desk and opened the envelope and spread out the birth certificates, report cards, diplomas, all kinds of things. She was just taking the cover off her mom's typewriter when the doorbell rang.

She rushed down the hall to let Angie in. But

when she opened the door, Angie was peering up the street.

"Look who's up there," Angie pointed. There was Lorraine, cycling slowly around in front of Mike's house.

"I wonder what she's up to." Kim stared for a minute, then shrugged. "Maybe she wants to show off her bike to Mike. Well, come on in. We've got lots to do."

She led Angie through the house to her mom's room.

"You don't think your mom will mind?" Angie stood in awe looking down at all the papers on the desk.

Kim felt a moment's uneasiness. Was that possible? "But it'll save her so much trouble. Besides, don't you think she'll like going to vet school?"

Angie frowned. "I don't know, Kim. I hear it's really hard. But your mom is sort of a bookworm type. She's always reading. I'd rather be a policewoman myself."

Kim smiled at Angie and wondered how she'd look in a police uniform with her dark frizzy hair and smiling brown eyes. "You'd be good, too," Kim said. "But come on. Let's get to work."

She rolled the application form into the typewriter, and Angie read her what was printed on the birth certificate. Kim typed carefully, using two fingers. Birthplace, Boston. Her mom had left Boston and her family fifteen years ago when Mr. Conway got his engineering job here in California. Later, Grandpa had died, then Grandma.

Next, Kim typed in her mom's social security number. Then Angie read the college diploma. "Bachelor of Arts in History, *cum laude*. What's that mean? Is it a sorority or something?"

Kim frowned. "No, I think it has something to do with good grades." She glanced at her watch. "Uh-oh. It's almost five. If Randy gets here, he'll blab this whole thing to Mom." She got up and peered anxiously out the window.

"Is Lorraine still there?"

Kim pressed against the windowpane. "Yes, she's still up by Mike's house. We'll have to walk that way to the mailbox, too."

She hurried back to the desk and picked up the form. "What should I do about this?" She pointed to a long vacant line, the place for her mom's signature. "Should I fake it?"

Angie looked alarmed. "What if they found out?"

"I know." Kim chewed her lip. "I wouldn't want to get her into any trouble. Sounds sort of like forgery, doesn't it?" She snapped her fingers. "I know. I'll just leave it blank. Forgetting is better than faking."

"Look, what about this?" Angie pointed to another blank space. "It says, 'Any special interests?'"

Kim frowned, thinking, then sat down at the typewriter again. Slowly she began to type. "I really like dogs a lot, and I had a police dog for many years and raised two sets of puppies."

She straightened up with a sigh. "Now it's all done."

"Good work." Angie smiled. "Maybe she will like it there."

"I hope." Kim folded the papers and put them in the self-addressed envelope. "Come on, Angie. Let's go mail this." She sprang to her feet, feeling suddenly excited. "Even if Lorraine is still out there."

They hurried out of the house and started up the street, passing Mrs. Greenberg and her white cat on the front porch. "Hello, Kim, how's your poor, dear mother?" she called out.

"She's fine, thank you, Mrs. Greenberg," Kim answered. Just wait till her mom was in vet school, then Mrs. Greenberg wouldn't be so pitying all the time.

Just then Angie groaned. "She's coming." Sure enough, Lorraine was pedaling her bike straight down the street toward them. "She's like some kind of a buzzard, waiting for someone to swoop down on."

Kim had to laugh. "I know. She shows up at all

the wrong times." She had told Angie about her trip to the pet clinic.

But now they reached the big blue mailbox, and suddenly Kim felt overcome by what she was doing. "Angie, should I really do this? Do you think Mom will mind?"

"How could she mind?" Angie raised her dark eyebrows in surprise. "You're only trying to help."

"Yes, that's true, isn't it?" Kim opened the lever on the mailbox and stuck the letter partway in. Go ahead, she told herself. It's a great idea. Mom will meet someone and laugh and smile and we'll be a real family again. She dropped the letter in the box and banged the lever shut.

"What're you two doing?" Lorraine spoke behind them. "How come it's taking you so long to mail a letter? Is it to a boy?" Lorraine squeaked her bike to a stop. It was a nice one, blue and silver. "That must be some letter if you can't decide whether to mail it or not," Lorraine said. Her eyes looked like two question marks.

Angie glanced toward Kim and let out an exasperated breath. "How come you're hanging around in front of Mike's house?"

"Well, as a matter of fact," Lorraine said calmly, "my mom was talking to his mom, and she invited our whole family to a party at their house." Lorraine looked very satisfied with herself. "Mom had to check it out first with my dad. He's really busy, you know."

Kim heard this news with a sinking heart. The Martineses were having a party, and she and her family were not invited? She watched as Lorraine circled her bike and pedaled off up the street.

"Don't worry, Kim," Angie consoled her. "You don't want to go if she's there, do you?"

"Oh, but I do." Kim exclaimed. "After all, Mike will be there." Besides, a party would mean her mom could go and wear her blonde wig and maybe meet someone.

10.
Larry the Laugh Riot

So I mailed it," Kim told Sara on the phone
Saturday morning. "Now all I have to do is
wait to hear from Southwest College."

"But, Kim," Sara protested, "that could be a
long time. Besides, you can't be sure your mom
will get in."

Kim didn't like to think about that possibility,
even for a minute. "I think she will."

"Well, listen, Kim, remember I told you about
my mom's *Singles* magazines? Why don't you
come over today and we'll look at them. Maybe
we could get a terrific idea for you. And we could
talk to my mom, too. She meets a lot of people in
her job at the restaurant. Maybe we could get
your mom a date right away."

"Sara." Kim stared delightedly into the phone.
"I'd love to. Mom's at the market with Randy. I'll
ask her as soon as she gets home."

A short time later, Kim was pedaling her bike

across town to Arbor Street, where Sara lived. With every passing moment she felt more hopeful, and when she turned onto Sara's street, the excitement rose within her. Maybe she and Sara could come up with something for tonight even. Maybe Mrs. Seeger really would have some suggestions.

At Sara's beige stucco apartment building, Kim rang the bell impatiently. A moment later, Sara's voice came through the intercom. "Kim?"

"Yes, I'm here, Sara."

With a click and a buzz, the apartment-house door opened, and Kim hurried inside. She raced up the steps to the second floor, where Sara was standing in the open doorway of her apartment. She was dressed in a fancy sweatshirt and tight pants, very stylish, like her mother's clothes.

"Hi," Kim said breathlessly. "I came as fast as I could. Sara, this is so fantastic."

Sara laughed. "I know. I'm excited, too." She combed her fingers through her short blonde hair. "Come on in. Listen, I found out Mom doesn't have her singles magazines anymore."

"She doesn't?" Kim felt a sinking disappointment.

"No, but she said people use the ads in the newspaper a lot these days." Sara led Kim over to the couch, in front of which was the coffee table, with the paper lying on top. "So let's look in there. I've already found some ads, and they are so fabulous."

"Sara, no kidding?" Now Kim's heart leapt up again. "What are they like?"

"They sound great, Kim. You know, we might be able to fix up your mom soon." For some reason, Kim felt a small doubt cross her mind, but she brushed it aside.

"Let's see, Sara." They both bent over the paper, which folded open to a long column of ads. Kim began to read: " 'Single? Meet someone special. Call us, 437-HUGS. Meet Singles, fun, exciting. Lonely? Call 971-CHAT.' "

"Sara, you're right. This is a good idea. I never thought to look in the newspaper." Kim felt a huge surge of hope as she read more ads, but she felt a little sadness, too. There were so many people looking for someone.

"Kim, look at this." Sara jabbed a pink fingernail at an ad that read: "Meet new friends through our Singles Message Center. Listen to messages, then leave your own."

Kim read it twice. "But I don't know, Sara, if Mom would do this."

"Of course. That's why you've got to do it for her. Here. Besides, we better hurry. Mom went to have lunch with Doug, you know, her boyfriend, and she's going to be back soon." Sara pulled the phone off an end table and handed it to Kim. "Just fake your voice, sound like an adult, you know?"

"Okay." Kim took the phone gingerly. It seemed suddenly too hot to touch. She lifted the receiver and listened to the dial tone, then hunching over the paper, she dialed the number. Sara crouched next to her and put her ear near the receiver, too.

A recorded woman's voice, warm and friendly, answered. "Welcome to our telephone message center. This is your introduction service to a new meaningful relationship in your life. Just listen to the following messages; then, at the sound of the beep, leave your own."

A man's voice came on the phone next. "Hi, there. I'm Jerry. I'd like to meet a nice lady and be friends with her." He did have a friendly voice, Kim thought. "We could go to a movie or dinner on the weekends. Call me at this number." He gave a phone number. "Or leave me your number."

Then a woman's voice came on. "Hello, I'm Carol. I'd like to meet some new friends. I have a two-year-old and I'm a little bit overweight, but I'm interested in lots of things, love to talk, and go to movies." She gave her phone number.

Then there was a silence followed by a beep. Kim's mind raced wildly. What should she do? She rolled her eyes worriedly at Sara.

"Talk like your mom," Sara whispered.

Kim nodded, gripped the receiver with a sweaty hand, and pursed her lips in an effort to sound like an adult. "Hi, uh, my name is Susan." If only her mom had a better name, like Amber. That was Mrs. Seeger's name. Kim went on. "I'm kind of small, with brown hair. I like to read and I like Chinese food and I speak a little French."

Kim suddenly thought of her dad's car accident. She couldn't let anything like that happen to her mom. "I don't like drunken drivers at all," she said firmly. That was true, too. Both she and her mom hated them. Kim had vowed she would never drink and drive, or date anyone who did.

"The phone number. Don't forget your phone number," Sara whispered.

"My telephone number is . . ." Somehow Kim couldn't go on. She tried to picture her mother getting a phone call from a strange man wanting a meaningful relationship. Would her mom like this?

Before Kim could do anything, Sara leaned toward the phone. "My number is . . ." and she rattled off Kim's number.

"No, Sara, wait, no." Kim slammed down the receiver. But it was probably too late. She stared at Sara, stricken. "Sara, maybe it isn't a good idea. I don't think Mom would like me to do this."

"Oh, Kim, it's a great idea. Really, it's terrific. But I'm sorry if you didn't want me to give your number."

Kim frowned. "I don't know, but anyway, maybe she won't get any calls."

Just then, the front door opened, and Sara's mother came hurrying in, her eyes bright, her jacket collar turned up in a stylish way. She looked like someone who'd have a name like Amber, Kim thought. "Hiya, kids. I just had lunch with Doug during his break." She shook off her jacket and ran her fingers through her short blonde hair, just the way Sara did. "Sure is a fun day. So how's everything going here?"

"Hi, Mom. Kim came over to spend the afternoon. Is that okay?"

Kim wondered if she and Sara looked guilty. What would Sara's mom think if she knew what they'd just done? Did it cost money to call the Singles Message Center?

"Sure, it's okay." Mrs. Seeger gave Kim a big smile. "I always like to have Kim visit. How's your mom doing?"

"Fine, thanks," Kim said, and wondered if she should admit her mom seemed sad.

"Kim's worried about her mom," Sara put in. "She doesn't have much fun, Kim thinks."

67

"Yes," Kim added. "She just comes home from work and doesn't go out or anything."

"Ah, that's too bad." Mrs. Seeger looked concerned. "I guess it was pretty tough, losing your dad like that, but it has been a while. . . . She should get out more and have a good time."

"I know," Kim agreed. "But I guess she doesn't get to meet many people, sitting at a desk and typing all day. It doesn't sound like fun, like your job."

"Yes, that's where Mom met Doug, in the restaurant," Sara put in.

"I wish something like that could happen to my mom," Kim said wistfully.

"Oh, that's a shame." Mrs. Seeger's face turned sad again. Suddenly, she snapped her fingers. "I've got an idea. Is your mom going to be home this evening?"

"She's always home, except when she goes to her French Club," Kim answered.

"Well now, listen, honey," said Mrs. Seeger, "tell your mom I'm going to be calling her, okay?"

"What's it about?" Sara asked.

"I just remembered. Doug said something at lunch about a friend of his coming to town tonight for a visit. He's a real funny guy. Doug always calls him Larry the Laugh Riot."

A little spark of hope started up in Kim's mind.

This sounded better, much better than getting a phone call from some stranger.

"He'll be needing a date, you see. I'll phone Doug about it right now, and you can ask your mom when you get home, Kim, okay? We'll be going to the Lake Street Grill at about six-thirty." Mrs. Seeger hurried across the living room and into her bedroom.

Kim was thrilled. She turned around and grabbed Sara and jigged up and down. "A date for my mom, Sara. Oh, how terrific! Thank you, Sara, for all your help."

11.
Blind Date

Kim pedaled her bike back toward home. She was bursting to tell her mom the good news. A blind date, Mrs. Seeger had called it, a date with Larry the Laugh Riot.

For a moment Kim wondered how it would be to have a dad who laughed all the time. Would he chuckle every morning as he shaved and showered? Would he laugh his way through dinner?

Anyway, her mom had a date, and Kim drew herself up proudly just thinking about what she'd arranged for her.

At last she turned onto Palm Street, quiet right now, its small elms beginning to drop a few yellow leaves. Looking down it, past the rows of stucco houses, she hoped to see Mike out in front of his house. But there was no sign of him.

As she biked down the street, she saw one person though — Lorraine's dad. He was sitting on his front step, hunched over a newspaper, his long legs stretched out before him. She slowed her bike and turned up her driveway, ready to call out, "Hello, Mr. Ridley," but he seemed so intent on his paper. She could see even from here that he had the paper open to the ads section. She wondered what it was he wanted to buy. Probably something wonderful for Lorraine.

Just then, Lorraine popped out the front door of her house, like a cuckoo out of a cuckoo clock.

Her father stood up, hastily folding his paper. "Hi, Punkin'," he said to her, and gave her a quick hug and went into the house. Seeing them together gave Kim a little ache in her chest.

"Hi, Kim!" Lorraine headed toward her. "Where've you been? I haven't seen you around today."

Kim felt like groaning. Lorraine, the tall, blonde spy. Did she have to know everything? "Over at Sara's," she said shortly, wheeling her bike up the driveway.

"Mike is playing soccer this afternoon. By the way, he says he's got some great new music to play at their party. Have you been invited yet?"

"No," Kim said abruptly. She tried to think of a quick defense. "Mom probably wouldn't have the time anyway." But why would Mike's mom invite Lorraine's family to a party and not hers? Did that mean Mike liked Lorraine?

"What're you going to do now?" Lorraine asked.

"Go in my house. My mom is expecting me."

"She looks busy to me. She's out in your back-yard, trying to mow the lawn." Lorraine pressed her lips together in that superior way of hers. "She could probably use some help, too."

How smug Lorraine sounded just because she had a father who could help her mother. Kim let out an annoyed breath. "My mom can handle things," she said shortly. Who wanted Lorraine's advice?

Kim parked her bike by the garage and hurried round to the back of her house. Let's see, what should she say and how should she say it? There was her mom bent over the lawn mower. Kim hurried over to her, ready to spill out her wonderful news, but something made her hesitate.

"Hi, Mom," she called out.

Mrs. Conway looked up from the lawn mower, a frown creasing her forehead. "Hi, dear. I'm having such trouble with this mower. Did you have fun over at Sara's?"

"Oh, yes, yes, I did."

Her mom turned back to the mower and Kim, looking down at her, noticed for the first time a few glints of gray in her brown hair. The sight shot fear through Kim's heart. Was her mom getting old, too old to date? Maybe she didn't have much time. She looked so worried as she bent over the mower that Kim wanted to say, "Please don't frown. Listen, Sara and her mom and I have the best idea for you."

But her mom stood up, her face flushed and annoyed-looking. "Would you run into the house and get me the screwdriver? It's in the kitchen drawer next to the refrigerator. And check on Randy while you're in there."

Poor Mom, Kim thought as she started for the house. Dad used to take care of things like a broken lawn mower. Why did they have to lose their dad? Why did it happen to them? Sometimes, she'd almost feel cross at him for going off and leaving them, but, of course, he couldn't help it. That was crazy of her to think that way.

In the house, she found the screwdriver and went down the hall to Randy's room. As she passed the phone, she thought about the Singles Message Center. How she hoped they wouldn't call today. She wasn't sure just how her mom would take it, and right now Kim wanted her to be in as good a mood as possible.

Randy was on the floor of his room, surrounded by the plates and pans from his stove. "Hi, Kim. Do you want something to eat?"

"No, not now, thanks. Have you heard the phone ring?"

"Uh-uh." Randy shook his head and dumped out a box of blocks on the floor.

Kim was relieved to hear that, and she hurried back outside to give her mom the screwdriver.

"Thanks, dear." Mrs. Conway bent down, put a metal piece back in the mower, tightened some screws, and stood up and turned on the mower. The engine sputtered, then rattled forth loudly. She smiled at Kim in triumph. "We did it," she called over the noise of the mower.

"Good for you." Kim was glad to see her mother in a better mood. "Want me to go in and set the table for supper?"

Mrs. Conway nodded and started pushing the mower off across the yard. Kim hurried back inside, eager to do everything that would keep her mom happy. When her mother came in, though, Kim would have to tell her about Larry.

In the kitchen, Kim put plates and glasses and silverware on the table, then folded napkins. She glanced at the clock. It was getting late.

A few minutes later her mother came in the back door, and just then, the phone rang. Uh-oh. Was it the Singles Message Center? Kim lunged for it. She knocked over a chair and crashed into the table.

"Kim, please," Mrs. Conway protested. "What's the big rush?" But Kim knew she couldn't possibly tell her.

She grabbed the receiver, ready to say, "You've got the wrong number" and hang up fast if it was

74

the Singles Message Center. But luckily it was Sara.

"You haven't called. Is everything okay?"

"Uh, yes, it will be," Kim said. "I'm sure it will." She shot a sidelong glance toward her mom.

"Good. My mom says it would be easier if Larry could stop by for your mom on his way over here."

"That'd be great," Kim said bravely. "Thanks, Sara."

Meantime, her mother had gone down the hall and into the bathroom. Kim followed her and listened outside the door. She heard the shower running. So that was good. Her mom was getting ready for tonight, though she didn't know it yet.

By the time Mrs. Conway came out of the shower, it was a little after six. Kim felt a mounting excitement, though a certain amount of apprehension, too, as she pushed open the bedroom door. Her mom was already pulling on her favorite old blue jogging pants.

"Hi, dear. I thought we'd have lasagna tonight. Do you want to get it out of the freezer?"

"Uh, listen, Mom." Kim leaned against the door. This was going to be harder than she'd thought, and she couldn't seem to get started.

Mom gave her a questioning glance. "No lasagna? Well, how about spaghetti and meatballs? I have some of that in the freezer, too."

"Mom, I don't care about meatballs." Kim began

to feel frantic. How could she tell her? She had to.

Now her mom was pulling on an old blue sweatshirt. "Well, okay. How about after supper we'll look at this stack of books I got from the library today?"

Ordinarily, Kim would be very interested. Her mom picked out great books. But she wished she'd stop talking about other things right now.

"I have to tell you something," Kim blurted out.

Mrs. Conway was brushing her hair now, and she shot Kim a blue-eyed glance in the mirror. "Could it wait just a minute . . ." She bent over to put on her shoes. ". . . while you run out to the freezer and get that spaghetti and pop it into the microwave?"

"But I . . . I can't go yet." Kim glanced nervously at the clock radio by the bed. Five minutes till Larry would come. How could time go so fast? "You see, when I was over at Sara's today, her mother was there. She's got this boyfriend, you know."

"Yes, you've told me before." Her mom had pulled on her shoes and straightened up. "What about him?" Did she sound a little impatient?

"Well, Mrs. Seeger is going out tonight to the Lake Street Grill."

Mrs. Conway let out a sigh and stood up. "That's a hangout for singles. You aren't going to ask me to go there, are you? I guess I'll just have to get that spaghetti myself." She crossed the room, brushed past Kim, and started up the hall.

"Wait, Mom. That's just what I told her, that you would go."

Mrs. Conway turned around and stared at her. "You what?"

"Yes, you see, she has this friend . . ."

Randy came running out of his room just then. "Where's she going?" he protested. "I don't want Mom to go anywhere."

At that moment, the doorbell rang. It was like an alarm clock, going off too early. Her mom didn't know about Larry yet, and she hadn't had a chance to get dressed or wear her blonde wig or that Spring Passion perfume or anything.

"Who can that be?" Mrs. Conway started back down the hall, and Kim rushed after her.

"I think it's the friend of Mrs. Seeger's. I didn't get a chance to explain. He's a lot of fun. They call him Larry the Laugh Riot."

Her mom threw her a startled look over her shoulder as she crossed the living room. "Larry the what?"

"Who is it?" Randy exclaimed, tagging along behind.

"Randy, be quiet," Kim told him crossly. If only there was some way to keep Randy out of sight. He'd scare off anybody. "It's a guy named Larry."

Mom was just reaching for the front door now. "He's Mom's blind date."

Mrs. Conway whirled around and stared at Kim in astonishment. "My what? Oh, Kim, really! What have you done?"

Shaking her head, her mom pulled open the front door. There on the step stood a reddish-faced man, blondish, sort of chubby, in checked pants and a shiny gray sports jacket. The jacket shone in the late afternoon sun and reminded Kim of the foil her mom wrapped around roasts in the oven. He was smiling.

"Hi, there," he said in a loud, hearty voice. "My name's Larry." He laughed. "Guess you heard I was coming, right? Ha-ha!" His face got even redder from the merriment of it all.

"Well, I, uh . . ." Kim's mother couldn't seem to go on for a moment. Then she said, "Would you, uh, like to come in?" She sounded polite, anyway, and Kim was relieved.

"Where's your big dog?" Randy pushed in front of Kim and looked out the door.

"Why, Randy?" Mrs. Conway asked. "What made you think he'd have a big dog?"

Randy screwed up his face the way he did when he was disappointed. "Kim said he was blind." He pointed at Larry.

Kim groaned. "Blind date, Randy. That means he and Mom don't know each other, not blind so he can't see. He is *so* immature," she apologized to Larry. Sometimes Mr. Chang used that word at school.

But Larry burst into loud guffaws. "Ho-ho. That's a good one. Ha-ha. He's a pretty bright kid. But say now . . ." He turned to Mrs. Conway. "Amber says you're going with us tonight. That's just great. We ought to have a good time at the Grill. The food's terrific, too." If he was worried about the way his date looked in her jogging pants and sweatshirt, he didn't show it.

Mrs. Conway gave him a really nice smile but she just stood there. "I'm so sorry. I just learned about this and, unfortunately, I had already made some other plans for tonight. I'm awfully sorry but I can't go with you. Would you be sure to tell Amber thanks ever so much for me?"

"Hey, are ya sure now?" Larry stopped smiling for a moment.

Mrs. Conway shook her head. "I'm afraid so. Maybe some other time, okay? And thanks a lot for stopping by for me."

And to Kim's stunned disappointment, Larry, in his foil-like jacket, was now backing out the front door, taking all his laughs with him. Kim had to blink her eyes hard to keep back her astonished tears. She could hardly believe this. What was the matter with her mother, anyway?

79

12.
Surfer Mailman

It took Kim days to get over her disappointment, even though her mom explained it several times.

"We just weren't right for each other, don't you see? We'd have different interests, and it wouldn't work out for him or for me. It really isn't good to be set up for these things. But thank you, dear, for worrying about me."

"But, Mom," Kim protested. "How can you tell all that about him when you don't even know him?"

But Mrs. Conway wouldn't discuss it any further.

And now, Kim worried, what would her mom do if she got a call from the Singles Message Center? Would she turn that down, too? Maybe not if it was the right person, someone like her dad. So maybe what she should do is screen the calls if there were any.

Every time the phone rang, Kim would make a rush for it until finally her mom said, "Kim, would you please slow down? The phone can't be that important."

"Oh, guess not. Sorry, Mom," Kim mumbled. But the truth was, the phone was very important. Those calls had to be checked.

It was a good idea, too, because one afternoon a call did come, luckily before her mom came home.

"Hello, there," a deep-voiced man said. "I'd like to speak to Susan. Is she your mother?"

"Yes, but she can't come to the phone right now." Mrs. Conway had told Kim never to let on that she was home alone.

"Do you think she'd like to go out and burn up the town some night?"

"Burn up the town?" Kim echoed. It didn't sound like her mother. "I doubt it."

"Well, would you tell her I've got a real fast car? We could really lay rubber."

He definitely didn't sound right for her mom. "She's, uh, she's, um, getting married next week." That was the end of that call. But now Kim realized that she'd have to keep on checking these calls.

Saturday morning at breakfast, her mother announced that she and Randy had a few errands to run. Kim was relieved. For a little while she could forget about the phone. Besides, she had other worries.

"Mike's parents are having a family party," she said to her mother. "Lorraine says they've already been invited."

"That's nice," Mrs. Conway said absently, slicing bananas.

"But we haven't been invited, have we?"

"Guess not." Her mother picked up a box of cereal. "Maybe they're still sending out invitations."

Kim felt more hopeful at the thought. "You could wear your new wig."

"My what?" Her mom looked up from slicing the bananas. "Oh, yes, dear, of course." Kim wished she sounded more excited. "Are you making friends with Lorraine?" Mrs. Conway added. "She could be lonesome."

"Lonesome?" Kim echoed. "It's hard, Mom. She's always boasting about things and telling me what to do."

Her mother shot Kim a quick glance, then smiled wryly. "Just be nice, then. They're our neighbors now."

But it wasn't easy trying to be nice to Lorraine. After her mom and Randy left, Kim decided to go out front and watch for the mailman. She hoped Lorraine wouldn't come buzzing out of her house. But then Kim heard the Ridley car backing out, and when she looked out the window, she saw Lorraine and her mother driving off in it.

So that was good luck. Kim hurried outside and settled on the front step. She sat looking up the street past the stucco houses. Mr. Ferraro was out front tossing a ball to his little boy again. How great that would be for Randy, Kim thought wistfully. If only he had a dad again. It'd be so nice for all of them.

From next door she heard the hum of the vacuum cleaner. Mr. Ridley must be cleaning the house. He was always doing a lot of helpful things. Last week he washed all the windows and he always did the yard work. How much easier it must have been for her mom when her dad was here.

Kim peered up the street again. At the far end of the block she saw the distant figure of the mailman. The big mail pouch slung on his shoulder looked stuffed. What kinds of letters did he have in it? Maybe there'd be one from Southwest College saying, "Dear Mrs. Conway, we think it would be wonderful if you took our pre-vet classes. . . ." Kim hugged her knees while she daydreamed that her mom would meet someone nice, like her old dad. She watched the blue-gray figure weave in and out of the front walks, stride, step, then plop something in a mail slot, then back out to the sidewalk again. Maybe he'd bring two letters today: "Dear Mrs. Conway, we're really hoping you and your family can come to our party. I'm looking forward to meeting all of you, especially your wonderful daughter. . . ."

Kim smiled, enjoying her fantasy, then frowned suddenly. She hoped Mike's mom wasn't cross about the way they had let the poodle escape.

The mailman kept pulling a folded magazine out of his pocket and reading it as he walked along. At last he was getting close. He tucked away his magazine, reached in his mailbag, and took out a bunch of letters. He went up to the Ridley's door and dropped the mail in the slot. Now he headed for Kim's.

"Hi." Kim rose quickly as he came up the walk. She didn't know his name, but he was always friendly, had longish blond hair, and eyes the same color as the blue-gray uniform.

"So, just hanging out today?" He smiled at her and thrust a stack of letters toward her.

"I was waiting for the mail," she explained. She took it from him and thumbed through quickly. There it was! A square envelope, decorated with autumn leaves, addressed to the Conway family, with the Martineses' name and address in the corner.

"Oh, wonderful!" she burst out.

"You like what you got?" He smiled.

"Yes, I do." She smiled back. "It's terrific!"

"Well, good." He pulled out his magazine and started to read it as he went down the steps.

"You must like to read," she said, watching him.

"Yeah, you bet."

Suddenly an idea began to smolder in the back of Kim's mind. "Does your wife like to read, too?" she asked cautiously.

He laughed. "Me? I don't have a wife. This is what I like to do." He held up the magazine cover showing a tanned muscular guy on a surfboard. "Well, got to get going." He went back down the front walk toward Mrs. Greenberg's house. Kim stood watching him as he went up to her door . . . *kaplunk* went the mail into the slot.

So he didn't have a wife and he liked to read; surfer magazines anyway. Her mom liked to read, too. What fun it would be to go to the ocean and take up surfing, though Kim couldn't quite picture her mother on a surfboard.

Kim jumped down the steps. "Wait," she called, and ran across the grass to Mrs. Greenberg's house. No time to think now. "Say, I was wondering . . ." She stood before the mailman and looked into his friendly face, so familiar, yet she didn't really know him; but too late now, the words came crowding out of her mouth. "Would you like to come for dinner at our house sometime?"

"Would I what?" The blue-gray eyes stared at her, surprised.

"Dinner — you know. I just thought, since you aren't married . . . my mom's a pretty good cook."

He smiled a little, looking down at her. "That's

nice of you, but, you know, I think you better ask your mom first, okay?"

"Oh, I will. I'll ask her today, then I could put a note out in the mail slot for you to let you know when. I know she'll love the idea."

When her mom finally came home, Kim raced to meet her. What a lot of good news she had!

"Look, Mom." Kim waved the invitation in the air. Even though it was addressed to all of them, she hadn't opened it. "Read it, Mom."

Her mother stepped out of the car, carrying some bundles, and frowned a little. "All right, Kim." She took the letter and undid the flap and slipped out an invitation. " 'Family open house,' " she read. " 'Please come Saturday, four to six on the sixteenth.' "

"Doesn't that sound great, Mom? We're all invited, aren't we?" The letter didn't say anything about "your wonderful daughter" but it was the same idea.

"Yes, it's very nice of them to ask us." Mrs. Conway started across the driveway. Kim wished she sounded more enthusiastic.

Randy climbed out of the backseat and slammed the car door. "I'm not going unless they have cake and ice cream."

"Listen, Mom, I've got some other good news, too." Kim reached into the back of the car and lifted out two more big bags. She followed her mother into the house and to the kitchen.

"I hope you won't mind, but I invited the mailman to come to dinner some night."

Mrs. Conway stopped, turned, and stared at Kim. "You did what?"

"The mailman, Mom. I asked him to dinner. Isn't that all right?"

"Who?" her mother echoed. She plopped the bags down on the table. Why did her mom have to look so surprised and cross all of a sudden, as if mailmen didn't eat, or shouldn't?

"You invited the mailman," Mrs. Conway repeated. A thin line creased her forehead.

"Well, yes, Mom. I mean, I saw him today." She described how she'd been waiting out front and he had come along.

"But, Kim, dear, I hardly even know him. I've talked with him sometimes on Saturdays, but that's all."

"Well, when I talked to him I found out he's not married and he likes to read the same as you, Mom. He was walking along, reading a surfing magazine. He's really into surfing, and you know how Randy wants to go swimming all the time."

"Kim! Really! Why, he must be half my age. Good heavens!" Mrs. Conway raised her hands to her head. "He probably thinks I put you up to it.

Honestly, Kim, you can't just go around asking strange men to dinner." She began to unpack one of the bags.

"But we sort of know him, don't we?"

"Well, hardly." She shook her head. "What in the world would we talk about? Surfing? I could ask him if the surf's up? Oh, Kim, Kim, our young mailman. Please, dear!"

"But, Mom, wouldn't it be good if we, uh, had another dad and we'd be like a real family again?"

"Nonsense, Kim, we *are* a real family. Now just stop trying to cook up things for me, all right? Just stop!"

Kim looked down at her hands and swallowed. It didn't sound very nice, the way her mother put it, that Kim was trying to "cook up" things for her, when actually all she wanted was for her mother to do a little cooking. Besides, certain things were already started, and there was no way Kim could stop them now.

13.
A Letter at Last

One of the things that Kim had started that couldn't be stopped was the application she'd mailed to Southwest College. Every day she checked the mail carefully, hoping for an answer.

Another thing she'd started was the call she'd made to the Singles Message Center. She didn't see how to end that, either, so she was constantly rushing to answer the phone before her mom could get it.

In the meantime, she worked hard on her career report, "Animal and Pet Care," sitting every night at her white wooden desk in her room. She'd been dying to have a desk a few years ago and still remembered her thrill when her dad had brought it home. "Now, you'll be a really good student, won't you?" He'd smiled at her as she'd opened all the drawers. Dad. Well, she was trying to make her report just as good as possible. She had persuaded her mom to read it and had mentioned several times what fun it would be to work as a veterinarian.

Her mom seemed interested, too. She kept saying, "That's great, Kim, and a very nice goal to work toward. It would be a very fulfilling career."

"Yes, don't you think so? I mean, really terrific." Kim wanted so much to add, "You'd like it, too, Mom." She wondered when they were ever going to get an answer from Southwest College. That would be the time to explain about the preliminary application form.

"Yeah, sounds good," Randy piped up. "Can boys be vets, too? I like dogs."

"Yes, you could, Randy." Their mom looked pleased. "We'll have two vets in the family."

Kim wished Randy would keep out of this. They couldn't all be vets.

Anyway, days went by after all the career reports had been handed in at school. Kim thought she'd done a good job, but she couldn't be sure. She knew Sara was worried about hers, too, and wondered if Mr. Chang would think it was good enough.

Finally, the day before the Martineses' party, Mr. Chang announced that he had read all the reports. "There were some outstanding ones." He smiled at the class, his dark eyes looking pleased behind his glasses.

Kim could feel herself go tense, and she saw

the worried look on Sara's face. But Lorraine was leaning forward on her desk, her blonde hair falling across her face, and she was wearing a proud expression. Probably Lorraine's was one of the ones Mr. Chang was talking about.

"In fact," Mr. Chang went on, "they were all so good I decided to have each of you give a quick oral report to the class."

Everyone groaned. "You'll like listening to them," Mr. Chang assured them.

Kim relaxed now, and she felt a surge of gratitude toward Mr. Chang. So they were all good. That meant hers, too, and Sara's. She shot a knowing glance toward Sara, who was smiling.

Mr. Chang went on. "I am hoping that you are thinking about these careers. As I said before, some day you'll be needed to help run this country. Have any of you thought seriously about that?"

Kim felt he definitely was looking in her direction, and a sudden hope swept over her. Why, yes, maybe she could actually be a vet herself when she grew up. Why not?

But now Lorraine had her hand up. "What about the picture of the winners in the paper?"

"Ah, yes," Mr. Chang said. "The newspaper photographer will be here next Wednesday to take pictures of those students. I'll announce them by then."

Kim felt a terrible pang of longing. If only she

could be one of them. Her mom would be so proud, and then she'd see how important it was to be a veterinarian.

After class, a lot of kids gathered around Mr. Chang, asking questions about who the winners might be. Lorraine wanted to know, "How should we dress, the ones who get in the picture?" as if she already knew she was a winner. She kept hanging around Mr. Chang, even though everybody else began to leave now, and as Kim went out the door, she saw Lorraine still talking busily to him.

Kim was still thinking about all this as she pedaled home on her bicycle after school. Angie had gone off to play soccer, and Sara went home on the school bus as usual. So Kim biked along alone, thinking about the career reports. What would it be like to be a vet some day, she wondered. Also, what would it be like if Lorraine got to be a winner and Kim didn't? Lorraine would really boast about it, Kim was sure. She'd have more advice to give than ever.

Kim was so busy with her thoughts that she didn't notice Mike come riding up behind her on his bike until he called out, "Hi, Kim."

She turned, startled but pleased to see his smiling face. "Oh, hi." How cute he was. "Have you washed any more dogs?" she asked.

"Hey, not yet. But soon as we get another good, dirty one, I'll call you."

"Okay." She laughed. She hoped that would happen. "I'd love to come down to your pet clinic again. We got the invitation to your party. It sounds like fun."

"Oh, yeah," he said. "We're having a whole lot of people. Mr. Chang is coming, too. The kids can go in the den and eat and listen to music. We're going to have some great food."

They rode slowly side by side on their bikes toward home and talked some more about the party and the pet clinic and about who might win the career contest. Kim nervously kept expecting Lorraine to come zooming up behind them on her bike at any moment. Lorraine would want to boast about her wonderful bike that she and her dad had rebuilt or her wonderful report or something. But luckily, she didn't show up, and when they reached Kim's house, Mike stayed around a little longer. Finally, he said, "See ya, Kim," and angled off on his bike down the street.

Kim went up her front walk, smiling to herself. It was definitely a plus to have Mike living nearby. It was too bad Lorraine did also. Just then, she glanced toward Lorraine's house and a strange thing happened. A white curtain in a front window seemed to sway for a moment. That's funny, Kim thought. Who could be home? She was sure she'd seen both Mr. and Mrs. Ridley drive off together in their car, the way they did every morning. She knew Lorraine couldn't be there yet. She was probably still back at school trying to impress Mr. Chang.

Then Kim spotted Mrs. Greenberg sitting by her window, her white cat on the windowsill, and Kim felt comforted by that. If anything was wrong, Mrs. Greenberg would have seen it. Besides, Kim decided, she must have imagined that the curtain moved. Kim waved at her neighbor, and Mrs. Greenberg picked up Peter's paw and waved it back. Kim smiled and went up her front walk. Peter was like Mrs. Greenberg's whole family, all she had. Pets were important to people, weren't they? Just think, some day *she'd* be taking care of people's pets, Kim thought with a sudden burst of pride.

Kim went into her house and scooped up the mail that had fallen from the mail slot onto the floor, then turned on some music. Mike's party was going to be fun. Maybe her mom would meet someone there, someone she would like, not as young as the surfer mailman, not as old and fat as Dwayne from the office, and not like Larry the Laugh Riot. It would be such a good chance for her to talk to Dr. John Martines and Dr. Lee Martines.

Kim thumbed eagerly through the mail. There it was at last, a letter from Southwest College! It was addressed to her mother, of course.

"Fab-u-lous," Kim shouted and danced around the living room. Still clutching the letter, she rushed back to her mother's room and looked at her dad's big framed picture.

"You'd think this was all right, Dad, wouldn't you? Mom isn't happy the way she is, and things are hard for her. Of course, no one could be as good a dad as you were. Whoever Mom meets would just be second best, always. But it'd be better for us, don't you think so, Dad?"

And she almost thought the silent face in the photograph looked at her with approval.

14.
End of an Idea

When Kim heard her mother at the front door, she snatched up the mail and ran to meet her. "Hi, hi," she said breathlessly. "Here's the mail. You want to look at it?" She thrust the letters into her mother's hands.

"Well, hi, honey. What's the big hurry?"

"Because this might be interesting." Kim pointed to the letter from Southwest College.

Mrs. Conway took the letter. "Is it something for your career report, Kim?"

"Well, not exactly. Please look at it." Kim was almost wild with impatience.

Looking puzzled, her mom opened the envelope and pulled out some papers and the very form Kim had filled out. Why were they sending it back? But there was a letter, too, and her mom began to read it aloud, frowning.

" 'Dear Mrs. Conway:
" 'If you would complete this preliminary

96

application form, sign it, send us a transcript of your college grades, and enclose an application fee, we could process your application for enrollment in course three-two-two in animal biology. . . .' "

She broke off. "Kim, I don't understand. What is this all about? Is it for your report? I thought you turned it in already."

"Yes, I did. Mr. Chang said today the reports were really good, and he's going to pick the winners soon. But, you see, I thought *you* might like to go to this class."

"Me? To college? To study animal biology?" Mrs. Conway looked amazed. "But — but why? We don't even have a dog or a cat."

"Because, it's a requirement for veterinary school. It's like a pre-vet course. And if you went there you might, uh, meet someone. Or later on, you could go to the vet school at the university."

A look of understanding broke across her mom's face. "Oh, Kim." Now she was smiling a big, amused smile. "You *are* trying to line me up with someone again! Come here, let me give you a hug."

"Well, sure, Mom." Kim submitted to the hug, but she didn't like the amused look on her mother's face. "But don't you think you might do it? They have night classes, and Mrs. Greenberg could stay with us."

97

"Kim, Kim." Her mother shook her head. "What a darling girl you are." She pulled off her jacket and reached out and patted Kim's hair. "That was a lot of work for you to fill out this application, wasn't it?"

"Well, yes, I guess it was. But it was worth it, Mom."

Randy came running out of the den and into the living room. "Hi, Mom. Come look at this ad on TV for the new zapper monster. Could you buy me one of those, please, please?"

Kim groaned. He *would* have to interrupt with one of his dumb ideas just then. "Randy, Mom and I are talking."

But luckily her mom wasn't interested in monsters. "No, Randy." She turned back to Kim. "I can't possibly attend college right now, either." She started toward the kitchen. "I have a lot of extra duties at the office these days, and we have so many bills to pay. Really, Kim, you shouldn't have bothered the college with such a wild scheme."

"What're you talking about college for?" Randy trailed after them. "Kim isn't even in high school."

"Randy, be quiet." Kim glared at him and hurried after her mother out to the kitchen.

"Mom, ple-e-ase, it's such a terrific idea. It'd be so good if you met someone — "

"Kim," Mrs. Conway interrupted, "if I went

back to school it would be because I wanted to learn something, not because I wanted to use it as a dating bureau."

"Yeah," Randy put in. "Mom doesn't need to go to school. So there!" He stuck out his tongue at Kim.

Kim wanted to shake him, but just then, the phone rang shrilly. Kim started to grab it, but her mom was closer and picked up the receiver before Kim could stop her.

"Yes," Mrs. Conway said. She listened intently, a frown line beginning to crease her forehead. "You're who?" she said.

Kim froze. Please, not now, she thought. This would not be a good time for a call from the Singles Message Center.

Then her mom said, "You're calling from where?" A puzzled look crossed her face. "The Singles Message Center? I did?" She sounded amazed. Randy had wandered out of the kitchen, and Kim wondered if maybe this wouldn't be a good time to go off to her room, too.

But her mom was speaking again. "Listen, I really don't know anything about this. Yes, I do speak a little French. Yes, I like Chinese food, but how in the world did you find out and how did you get my number?"

Suddenly Mrs. Conway shot a quick, knowing glance at Kim. "Well, look, thanks very much for calling. But, no, thanks a lot. I'm uh, really tied up — yes, permanently."

Her mom hung up and Kim felt a wave of apprehension. Was she going to be very cross?

"Kim, do you know something about this Singles Message Center? Did you give out our phone number?"

Kim looked down at the floor, trying to decide what to say. Finally, she took a deep breath and raised her head. "Yes, Mom. You see, when I went over to Sara's . . ." and she told her all about calling the Singles Message Center. "But I said you'd never go out with anyone who drank and drove a car. That way I thought you'd get the right kind of person."

Mrs. Conway shook her head, still frowning, but at least she didn't look really angry. "You've just got to stop all this, Kim. You understand? It really wasn't such a good idea to give out our number either. I know you mean well but stop worrying about me. Now I must go change and start dinner."

She turned and walked down the hall to her room, but Kim couldn't help following her. "But, Mom, Sara and I thought the Singles Message Center was a really fabulous idea."

The phone rang again, and this time Mrs. Conway hurried across her room to answer it. Kim held her breath, fearing the worst. It couldn't be another call from the Singles Message Center, could it? Not right now.

But her mom was smiling as she spoke into the phone. "Hi, Jan. Yes, I can chat for a few minutes." She sank onto her bed. Over the receiver she said to Kim, "Would you go out and start setting the table, dear?"

Kim left the room, but she didn't go right to the kitchen. She just stood in the hall for a minute, trying to figure it all out. She felt confused and upset. Whatever was the matter with her mother, turning down one good idea after another?

Then, unbelievably, she heard low laughter coming from the bedroom, and she heard her mother saying, "Yes, veterinary school, can you imagine that? Yes, yes, it is pretty funny, isn't it? And then the Singles Message Center called." More laughter. Kim rushed off down the hall to the kitchen and began to bang the silver loudly down on the table. To be laughed at, that was the worst of all! What was the matter with her mother? Why did she think it was all so funny? Why couldn't she see what good ideas these really were?

Kim opened the refrigerator, then slammed it shut. Well, she wasn't going to give up now. Tomorrow at the party at Mike's house, maybe his parents could talk her mom into going to vet school.

15.
Please Try

When Kim woke up the next morning, the first thing she thought was, Today is the party. She lay, smiling for a moment, watching the yellowing leaves on an elm outside her window. The party was going to be so great. She'd get to see Mike and maybe Mr. Chang. Would he know who the winners in the career contest were? Would he tell?

She heard her mother's footsteps in the hall, heard the bathroom door close. Kim turned over restlessly in her bed. Surely her mother would wear her plum-colored dress tonight and her wig, of course. She herself would wear her best skirt, blue like the sky, with its matching blue-and-white blouse.

As she lay there, she realized her mother was going back and forth to the bathroom. Why? What was going on? Somehow it didn't sound quite right. She jumped up out of bed and hurried down the hall to her mother's room. Her mom was back there now, back in bed, too, her face buried in the pillows. She looked so small under the covers in that big double bed.

"Mom, how come you're still in bed?"

Her mother groaned. "I don't feel well, Kim. It's my stomach, something I ate or a flu bug, I don't know which."

"Oh, that's terrible. What about the party?"

Mrs. Conway groaned again. "I know. I haven't forgotten."

"What can I do? Want me to get you some tea or a soft drink?" Her mom had to get well, she had to!

Throughout the day, Kim did everything she could. She fixed her mom tea and chicken broth and made meals for Randy. It was always a little scary to have their mother get sick. When that happened, sometimes Kim couldn't help thinking the worst. What if she couldn't go to work anymore? Who would take care of them then? They'd lost a dad, so mightn't they lose their mom, too? That was the scariest thought of all.

But today Mom isn't very sick, Kim told herself, and she'd probably be okay by this afternoon. She had to be. Kim took Randy off to the park for a while, so the house would be quiet and their mom could rest.

When they got back, Mrs. Conway was still in bed, sound asleep. Kim decided she'd get herself dressed first for the party. She went to her room and pulled on the blue skirt and blue-and-white striped blouse. The blue even matched her eyes, she thought, as she leaned toward the mirror and peered excitedly at herself. This was going to be such a great party.

From outside, Kim could hear the steady *thud thud* of a ball Randy was throwing against the garage door. Randy should be coming in and getting ready, too, Kim thought, but first she'd see about her mom. She tiptoed down the hall to the bedroom doorway.

"Mom," Kim whispered.

This time her mom pushed the pillows off her face and opened her eyes. "Hi, dear."

"How are you?"

Mrs. Conway half sat up, her brown hair a tousled mass around her head. "Well, I think I'm better."

"Oh, good." Kim smiled. "That's great. It's almost time to leave for the Martineses' party."

"Oh, yes. How nice you look, honey. My pretty Kim." She smiled at Kim, then glanced at her bedside clock. "I've slept such a long time. Thank you for taking care of Randy all day. You've been a big help."

"Yes, but now we should be going. The party's from four to six, the invitation said. Do you want me to get out Randy's good clothes? I'm all dressed."

Why wasn't her mother getting up? Why did she just keep sitting on the edge of her bed in her wrinkly nightgown?

She yawned wearily. "Kim, I just don't think I'm up to it."

"Mom, please try. Here I'll help you. I can get out your clothes for you, too. You're wearing that plum-colored dress, aren't you? And just think, now you can wear your blonde wig."

"Oh, uh, yes, I guess I could, couldn't I?" Mrs. Conway said in a kind of strangled voice. At least she did stand up then, wearily pushing her hair off her forehead. Kim hurried over to the closet. But then her mother said, "Kim, don't bother, I really can't go."

Kim turned to stare at her mother. "What? You can't go?"

"Yes, dear, my stomach is still too queasy. It'd be hard to face all those people feeling this way, and Randy will be better off at home, too."

"But, Mom, you said you were better. You've been resting all day. I've been planning on going for weeks and weeks." Kim glanced toward the window and just happened to see Lorraine Ridley and her parents walking past on their way to the party. Kim caught a glimpse of a red ribbon in

Lorraine's blonde hair and saw that her dad was wearing a dark jacket and a necktie.

"Mom, we *have* to go." Didn't she realize what a good chance this might be to meet someone? And talk to Mike's parents about vet school? "This is just not very fair!"

"I'm sorry, Kim. But you can still go. I'm sure that would be all right with Mike's parents. Just be certain to come home before dark."

"I have to go by myself?" Kim thought of how the others would be there with their families. Suddenly, she felt something like a ball of fire start up in the pit of her stomach. Everything she'd planned, everything she'd tried to do was just falling apart.

And now her mother was putting on her bathrobe. She didn't even look very sick, either. Kim couldn't keep quiet any longer. "Mom," she burst out, "I don't see why you couldn't go for a little while. You never want to go anywhere or do anything. It's all so quiet and lonesome around here ever since Dad died and . . . and I hate the way it is. All you ever do is say no, no to everything. Can't you ever say yes?"

"Why, Kim!" Her mother looked up with a startled face.

"It's not right," Kim went hurtling on, her voice rising. "I heard you laughing about me on the phone yesterday when you were talking to Jan.

All you do is say no to all my ideas. You didn't like the Singles Message Center or Larry the Laugh Riot or the mailman coming to dinner. And then all you do is just sit around at home and you don't do anything."

"Sit around?" her mother echoed.

Kim could feel her face getting hotter and hotter and tears rushing to her eyes. But she couldn't stop, even though her mom's face looked shocked and pained now. "You don't even try. You don't try at all. You might meet some nice man at the party. Anyway, you could at least talk to Mike's parents. They could tell you all about how they met in vet school. We need a dad, can't you see that? Then we'd be a real family again, with a mother and father, the way we used to be, the way we ought to be. Oh, why can't you help more?"

"Now, Kim," Mrs. Conway started to say, but Kim was past listening now. Angrily, she whirled around and headed for the door.

"So I'll go, all right, and *all by myself.*" She flung herself out of the room and down the hall and out the front door. She slammed it good and hard behind her.

16.
A Bad Afternoon

Voices and music poured out of the windows of the Martineses' house, and a bunch of bright autumn leaves decorated the front door. Some people were gathered there, about to go in, and Kim hurried up the walk to join them. She could slip in with them, pretend to be part of that family, whoever they were.

But, unfortunately, Dr. Lee Martines, dressed in a long yellow skirt and a puffy white blouse, and Dr. John Martines in a bright green jacket, were right inside the door, greeting people as they came in. Kim tried to slip past them, hoping to avoid questions about the rest of her family.

But as she was taking off her jacket, Dr. Lee Martines spotted her. "Kim, how are you?" she called out.

"Oh, fine, fine thank you, Dr. Martines." Kim tried to smile, to sound as if that were true. Actually, she felt terrible, as if she had a great weight hanging over her. She couldn't remember ever yelling at her mother like that. Now Dr. Martines was sure to ask her questions, like, "Where's your mother, Kim, and your father?"

But, oh, what luck — a man came up to Mike's parents and started talking to them. Kim quickly dropped her jacket on a pile of coats and eased into the living room. The room was jam-packed with people, all laughing and talking and having such a good time. Was the whole world happy except for her and her mother, Kim wondered.

She decided to find Mike. She saw his dark, curly hair in the crowd, and just seeing him lifted her spirits for a tiny moment. But he was with Lorraine, and they were both talking to Mr. Chang.

Kim started across the room. She wished she could ask, "Mr. Chang, please, could you tell me, am I one of the winners of the career contest?" But maybe he hadn't even decided yet.

As she slipped through the crowd, eager to get over to Mike, she kept overhearing scraps of other people's conversations. She got halfway across the room and then found herself firmly blocked by the backs of several women. One of them was tall with tightly waved blonde hair. It was Mrs. Ridley. Kim especially didn't want to see her and have her asking a lot of questions about where her mom was. Kim didn't dare try to push past her. But now several other people had moved in behind her, and she couldn't budge.

As the voices around her rose and fell, Kim couldn't help hearing some of their conversations. A woman was leaning toward Mrs. Ridley and speaking softly in her ear, but still, Kim heard her words, something about Mr. Ridley. Kim heard the woman say, "How's Ben doing? Has he had any luck?" Lorraine sometimes called her father by his first name, Ben. Kim wondered what kind of luck Mr. Ben Ridley was hoping for.

Mrs. Ridley turned to the woman then and said in a low voice, "No, none at all. There just don't seem to be any jobs out there for him. He's been out of work for a year now. He's so ashamed. He keeps trying to hide it from everyone. He leaves the house each morning when I do and he stays away all day."

The men behind Kim laughed loudly at something, and the rest of Mrs. Ridley's words were lost. But Kim had heard enough to be astounded. Mr. Ridley was looking for a job? He wasn't this important, busy consultant Lorraine was always boasting about?

The men shifted behind her, and Kim saw an opening to ease through and get away from there. She was so embarrassed. She knew she'd heard something she wasn't supposed to hear. Still, it wasn't her fault, she told herself. She couldn't help it, but she couldn't forget it, either. There was no way to wipe it out of her mind.

So braggy Lorraine didn't have such a perfect family after all. Just think, she had been lying to cover up for her dad. But somehow it didn't seem like such a bad thing to do. Lorraine was just trying to protect him. Kim knew what it was like to love your father.

Kim pushed past some other people, but she didn't see Mike anymore. Lorraine was now across the room, standing with her dad. She was busily talking and talking to him. He just stood there listening, his head tipped in her direction, his bald spot gleaming in the overhead lights. He didn't seem to be saying much and he looked sad. Poor Mr. Ridley. Other families had problems, too, Kim realized suddenly.

Then Kim spotted the doorway into the den, and peering in, she saw the room was full of boys and girls. She edged in, looking for Mike. He was bending over, putting a tape into a tape deck and turning up the music, then talking to some older boys whom Kim didn't know. A couple of teen-agers began to snap their fingers and dance. Kim didn't want to barge into that group around Mike, so she looked around and saw two girls from school sitting on the couch — Jannelle and Anna.

"Hi," Kim said to the girls, going over to them. "It's a great party, isn't it?"

"Sure, terrific," Janelle agreed, and then both slid over to make room for Kim. For a little while they sat, listening to the music and eating chocolate chip cookies from a plate on the coffee table. Mike had said he was going to make these for the party, and they were big and fat and delicious.

But now Mike was through talking to those boys, and Kim stood up and started toward him. "Hi, Mike," she called out.

He turned, and when he saw her, he beckoned to her urgently. "I've got something to tell you. Come on over here."

She followed him to a corner of the room, away from the others, wondering what he wanted to talk about. "What is it, Mike?" She felt mystified.

He leaned toward her, his dark eyes excited. "Listen, this is a secret, so don't tell anybody yet. But I was just talking to Mr. Chang." Suddenly, Kim knew what the news was. He must be one of the winners. She felt glad for him, but a surge of sadness for herself.

But Mike was still talking. "He says we're going to have our picture in the paper next week, Lorraine . . ." Of course she'd known Lorraine would be one of the winners. " . . . and me and . . ." He paused. " . . . and you."

Kim stared into his eyes, stunned. "Me? Oh, Mike, do you really mean it?"

Mike nodded. "That's right. He said he went over the career reports some more this morning, and we're part of the top group."

"*Fabulous*," Kim cried with delight. "How terrific, terrific! Oh, Mike, thanks for telling me. And congrats to you, too."

Just then, the boys called to Mike, and he turned to go. "Those are my cousins," he explained. "I better see what they want. But wait here, would you? I want to ask you something."

After he left, Kim just stood there, smiling to herself. She was so excited. She wished she could go over and tell Anna and Jannelle, wished she could shout it to the whole roomful of people. But Mike had said not to tell.

Just think — she, Kim Conway, had written one of the top reports and would be having her picture in the paper! Maybe someday she'd really be a veterinarian. Yes, she would — for sure! Meantime, her mother would be so impressed, she might think again about taking that pre-vet course. But remembering her mother brought back that heavy feeling. And hearing all the hum of music and happy voices made Kim think she ought to go home now and see how her mother was feeling. What did she think about all those terrible things Kim had said to her?

Kim eased through the crowd toward Mike, wondering what it was he still had to say to her. "Mike, I think I better leave now," she called to him.

"Wait, Kim, wait." He pushed through the knot of boys and came over to her. "Do you have to go so soon?"

"Yes," she said, "but thanks a lot for inviting me to your party. Would you thank your parents, too, in case I don't get to see them? My mom's sick, you see, so I better go home."

"Hey, too bad. Did you just come with your dad then?"

With a start, Kim realized Mike didn't even know she had no dad. But why would he? She'd never told him. She never told anyone if she could help it. But now, somehow it didn't seem like that difficult a thing to do. "My dad's dead, Mike," she said simply. "He was killed in an auto accident almost three years ago."

A look of sympathy crossed Mike's face. "I'm sorry . . ."

"What did you want to ask me, Mike?"

"Oh. Yeah. My parents say they'll be short-handed again on Monday, and I wondered if you'd like to come to the clinic and help me walk a couple of dogs who've been boarding there."

"Oh, yes, yes, I'd love to." She gave him a big

smile and turned to leave. "That'd be terrific fun. But now I have to go."

She threaded her way back through the crowded rooms. Mike's parents were on the far side of the dining room and too hard to get to, so she just picked up her jacket from the chair by the front door and let herself out of the house. She had to talk to her mother.

17.
Surprises

Kim fastened her jacket and hurried down Palm Street, leaving the noise and the voices and the music behind her. She passed a row of empty parked cars and shivered a little. Was it because of the late afternoon coolness or because she felt tense? How was her mother feeling? Cross, upset, sad?

Kim's mind went back to what she'd heard about Mr. Ridley. The poor Ridleys. And look at her own family — why, they were lucky in a lot of ways. Her mom had a good job, at least.

She raced up her front walk, but when she reached the front door, she leaned against it for a minute. It was silent inside, not like all the noise and music at the Martineses', but it felt good to get home.

She opened the door quietly. She didn't hear a sound. Maybe her mom had put Randy to bed early and had gone back to sleep herself.

Kim crossed the living room on tiptoe and

116

started down the hall. But the light was on in her mom's room and Mrs. Conway called out in a surprised voice, "Is that you, Kim?"

Kim was relieved. At least her mother didn't sound cross. "Yes, I'm home." Kim paused in the doorway. There was her mom, sitting up in bed, and she had some letters spread out on the blanket beside her. She looked up at Kim with a serious expression on her face.

"Kim, I'm glad you're back. We really need to have a talk."

"Yes, oh, yes we do!"

"Ever since you left, I've been thinking about what you said," Mrs. Conway added. "I'm afraid we haven't been understanding each other."

"I guess that's right. Oh, Mom, I'm so sorry." Kim darted across the room and flopped on the floor by the bed and buried her face in the covers. "I kept remembering the mean things I said to you," she went on in a muffled voice. "I guess I was just all mixed up or something." Leaning against the bed, she suddenly felt very tired. It had been a busy day. "I know you work so hard to take care of us and . . . and it's great you have a good job and all."

"There, Kim." Her mom reached out and began to stroke her hair. "You were upset and disappointed with me about the party. Parties with the neighbors are still a little hard to take. Some of the neighbors know about Dad, and their sympathy kind of brings it all back."

"Yes, I know." Kim remembered that look on Mike's face when he heard she didn't have a dad. "Mom." Now she looked up at her mother. "I heard this woman talking to Mrs. Ridley." She told her mother what she'd heard about Mr. Ridley being without a job.

"And all this time Lorraine has been boasting and boasting about her dad's great job. I thought about you, Mom, and how you've been taking such good care of us ever since Dad died — " Kim broke off. Poor old Lorraine, telling lies and bragging about what wasn't true.

Mrs. Conway nodded thoughtfully. "Too bad. I suspected something like that. Lots of families have problems at some time or another, you know. I was really sorry not to go with you tonight. I just didn't realize it meant so much to you that I go."

"I was hoping you could talk to Mike's parents and hear how they met in vet school," Kim confessed.

A look of understanding broke across her mother's face. "You really do want me to find another dad for you and Randy, don't you?"

"Well, I thought it'd be easier and better for all of us. We'd be a real family again."

Her mother closed her eyes for a moment as if

she were remembering. Then she opened them. "At least we had a wonderful dad once, didn't we? But it'd be hard to find another one as good, and I haven't felt quite ready for that. When I do meet someone new, it'll have to be through my own friends and activities, not dating services or blind dates with people who aren't like me. You see, dear? Meantime, we have one another and our nice home here. There are a lot of good things to be thankful for. In fact, I have some news."

Then Kim remembered that she did, too. How could she have forgotten her wonderful news in the midst of all this? "Oh, me, too. Guess what?" She jumped up from the floor and bounced down on the edge of the bed. "I'm a winner in the career contest. Mike found out from Mr. Chang, and he told me we're going to have our picture in the paper. Some day I think I will be a vet, like Mike's parents."

Her mom laughed. "Oh, Kim, that's wonderful! I knew your report was excellent. Congratulations."

"What's your news, Mom? Is Aunt Ruth coming?"

Her mother was smiling now in such a very special way. "No, afraid not. But after you left, I went through the mail that came today. I had heard about a very exciting new job." She picked up a letter from the bed and held it up. "This came today with further details. A big company needs a new office manager, and they say I have a very good chance."

Kim stared at her mother. Her blue eyes were shining, and her whole face looked so absolutely radiant.

"Why, Mom, how great."

"Yes. It'll be more challenging and interesting than my old job, and, Kim, I've promised them I'll take a course in business, probably one evening a week, to prepare."

"Why, Mom, this is all terrific." Kim couldn't get over the way her mother looked. To think she could be so happy about a new job. But why not? There were lots of ways to be happy in this world, weren't there?

Suddenly, Kim had an idea. She jumped up and rushed to the closet and pulled the blonde wig off the shelf. "Look, Mom, you could wear this to your new job." She handed it to her mother.

Her mom nodded slowly. "Well . . . I suppose I could." She put it on her head, tucking her hair under it. "How do I look? Would this be good for the new office manager?"

Just then, they heard a noise from Randy's room, and he came shuffling in, wearing his dinosaur-print pajamas, his brown hair all mussy, his eyes blinking in the light. "I've been waiting and waiting for you, Mom. You were going to come and read to me," he said accusingly.

"I know, dear. I did come, but you were asleep."

Randy came over to the bed, looked up at Mrs. Conway, and screwed up his face. "Yukky. You're wearing that funny hat thing again. You look like a monster."

"Oh, Randy," Kim said impatiently. But as she stared at her mom's glowing face, she realized that the wig didn't look quite right. It was too shiny, too unnatural, not like her mother at all. Now Kim wondered if she'd been wrong, trying to get her to wear it. Maybe she'd been trying to make her mother lead a different kind of life, to do things that weren't right for her. Maybe she'd been a little bossy, like Lorraine, trying to run other people's lives.

"You know, Mom, I don't really think you need that wig. Why don't you take it off?"

"Well, it is rather hot." Her mother lifted off the wig and shook out her brown hair.

"Yay-y-y! Now you look like my mom," Randy exclaimed.

"Yeah, he's right," Kim agreed, putting her arm around her brother. "You do look better without it." And as she looked at her mother's happy face, she knew now they could be a real family just the way they were.

APPLE°PAPERBACKS

Pick an Apple and Polish Off Some Great Reading!

NEW APPLE TITLES

❑	MT41917-X	**Darci in Cabin 13** Martha Tolles	$2.75
❑	MT42193-X	**Leah's Song** Eth Clifford	$2.50
❑	MT40409-1	**Sixth Grade Secrets** Louis Sachar	$2.75
❑	MT41732-0	**Too Many Murphys**	
		Colleen O'Shaughnessy McKenna	$2.75

BESTSELLING APPLE TITLES

❑	MT42709-1	**Christina's Ghost** Betty Ren Wright	$2.75
❑	MT41042-3	**The Dollhouse Murders** Betty Ren Wright	$2.50
❑	MT42319-3	**The Friendship Pact** Susan Beth Pfeffer	$2.75
❑	MT40755-4	**Ghosts Beneath Our Feet** Betty Ren Wright	$2.50
❑	MT40605-1	**Help! I'm a Prisoner in the Library**	
		Eth Clifford	$2.50
❑	MT41794-0	**Katie and Those Boys** Martha Tolles	$2.50
❑	MT40283-8	**Me and Katie (The Pest)** Ann M. Martin	$2.50
❑	MT40565-9	**Secret Agents Four** Donald J. Sobol	$2.50
❑	MT42883-7	**Sixth Grade Can Really Kill You**	
		Barthe DeClements	$2.75
❑	MT42882-9	**Sixth Grade Sleepover** Eve Bunting	$2.75
❑	MT41118-7	**Tough-Luck Karen** Johanna Hurwitz	$2.50
❑	MT42326-6	**Veronica the Show-off** Nancy K. Robinson	$2.75
❑	MT42374-6	**Who's Reading Darci's Diary?** Martha Tolles	$2.75

Available wherever you buy books...
or use the coupon below.

- -

Scholastic Inc., P.O. Box 7502, 2932 East McCarty Street, Jefferson City, MO 65102

Please send me the books I have checked above. I am enclosing $_____ (please add $2.00 to cover shipping and handling). Send check or money order — no cash or C.O.D.'s please.

Name_____

Address_____

City _____ State/Zip _____

Please allow four to six week for delivery. Offer good in the U.S.A. only.
Sorry, mail order not available to residents of Canada. Prices subject to change.

APP589